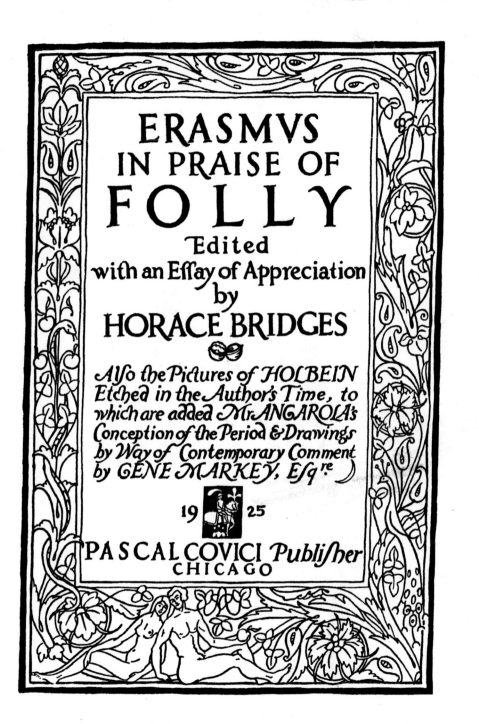

ERASMVS
IN PRAISE OF
FOLLY
Edited
with an Essay of Appreciation
by
HORACE BRIDGES

Also the Pictures of HOLBEIN
Etched in the Author's Time, to
which are added Mr. ANGAROLA's
Conception of the Period & Drawings
by Way of Contemporary Comment
by GENE MARKEY, Esqre

19 25

PASCAL COVICI Publisher
CHICAGO

ERASMVS
Aº 1466–1536 Dᵗ

To

JOE AND ALBERTINE,

as a souvenir of many delightful literary and other foregatherings, this edition of an ever-living classic is affectionately dedicated by

THE EDITOR.

LIST OF ILLUSTRATIONS

INTRODUCTION IN PRAISE OF

ERASMUS

§ I.

THE FAMILIAR PHRASE about the history of the world being the judgment of the world is a deadly and detestable heresy, if it is taken to mean either that whatever has happened was bound to happen, or that the mere fact of a cause having been lost is proof that it was never worth winning or dying for. ¶ I do not deny that the German apophthegm may be patient of another and a truer construction. The objection to it is precisely its lack of precision, its Delphic vagueness. A saying that may mean anything actually means nothing. ᵥ Many causes have failed that ought to have succeeded, and the world may have to retrace its steps over more than one travelled road. Where this is impossible, it may still be our duty to recognize that past errors have made present conditions poorer than they need have been, and subjected the nations to suffering and loss that could have been escaped.

These reflections should stand at the head of any appreciation of the glorious Erasmus of Rotterdam, since his life was one long losing fight, one endless victory in defeat and defeat in victory, for the great-

est of all lost causes. This was a cause better worth
losing than any other in that age was worth winning. It was a cause that lifted its elect minority of
advocates above the smoke and stir of their time, and
united them with the far past and the distant future.
It was the attempt to preserve a principle and an
ideal indispensable to the perfection of humanity,—
a principle and an ideal, the obliteration of which in
men's consciousness was the major cause of the con-
fusions, wars, and travails of the ensuing four centuries; a principle and an ideal to which mankind
is painfully endeavouring to struggle back, in the
assurance, hammered by stern experience into the
subconsciousness of the race, that only by building
on that principle and orienting society towards that
ideal can the possible efflorescence of the genius of
man be attained, amid the secure peace which is at
once its indispensable condition and its crowning
glory.

The principle was that of *the moral and spiritual
unity of the human race:* that we truly are one body
of many members, the very diversity of which, alike
in structure and in function, is but the out-working
of a single life-energy, and instrumental to the fulfilment of a common purpose, the attainment of a
common destiny. √ The more the members of the one
body (individuals, families, vocations, nations) are
individuated and differentiated, the greater becomes
the need of reciprocal interaction between them, and
the more imperative the creation or maintenance of
a central organ to mediate their interaction and re-

mind them of their interdependence and their common destiny. ✓

Such was the principle. And the ideal was the reformation, *without destruction*, of that great international organization which, first as the Roman Empire and later as the Roman Church, had been for Europe the source, reservoir, and soul of civilization. The source,—because it had put law, order, union and communion in the place of barbarous anarchy and disunion; the reservoir,—because in and through it had been conserved and 'treasured up on purpose to a life beyond life' the spiritual streams flowing from those twin headwaters of our civilization, Palestine and Greece; and the soul,— because, holding within it these principles of life, it was able, even amid the wreck of its own imperial structure, to avert their extinction, to preserve their vitality, to sustain them latent yet living through the long night of sleeping generations and unconscious centuries;—to be thus truly

the prophetic soul
Of the wide world dreaming on things to come;

—and, in Humanity's favouring hour, to bring them forth from its treasury and make them the nurturing substance of a new, and potentially a nobler, civilization.

§ II.

The task, then, was to preserve this indispensable element at the heart of the Roman Church— namely, its unfulfilled prophecy of Catholicism (for

more than an unfulfilled prophecy, lamentably remote from fulfilment, it never has been, and is now
least of all). And the first thing necessary to this
end was to attack the actual Church. For the Church
was a huge organization and concentration of power,
in hands that had long since become irresponsible;
and power irresponsible is but a periphrase for power
abused.

Functions neglected; disciplinary rules ignored and
forgotten; a vast governmental system of extortion
substituted for what should have been a system of
super-national service and succour; insolent and
domineering ignorance usurping foundations intended for labour and social service; unspeakable and in-
describable vice and sottishness in the very refuges
built for virtue and idealism; Rome itself a sink of
iniquity, graft, robbery, assassination and all pollu-
tion; Borgia Popes; a Tammanyized cardinalate and
episcopate; all branches of the clerisy debauched,
simonized, profligate; the whole organization, in each
land and internationally, rotten with politics in the
worst American sense of that degraded word; a
clergy immune from secular justice, and responsible
only to corrupt ecclesiastical courts that always
favoured them, no matter what their crimes; and a
laity condemned—nay, compelled—to accept and
practice a vast system of fetishistic superstition in
place of the predominantly ethical religion of Jesus
and St. Paul: such was the frightful parody of a
Catholic Church on which the eyes of Erasmus gazed

IN PRAISE OF ERASMUS

as he wandered over Europe at the end of the XV
and the beginning of the XVI century.

And let the reader note well, that this account of
the unreformed Church is no invention of its enemies,
but the indisputable testimony of faithful sons, who
hoped against hope that its universal corruption
might be cleansed and purged away, so that its essential values might be released and made of service to
the new Europe, which was coming to birth in the
form of a galaxy of nations. Every count in the
indictment can be proved to the hilt out of the writings of Erasmus and countless other loyal Catholics
before his time, without summoning a single Protestant witness to the bar.*

Attack, therefore, was indispensable. The Church,
in Tyrrell's striking phrase, was 'in the grip of the
hawk', and when has the hawk—especially where
his name is Legion—been dislodged from the quarry
without a struggle? But there are two modes of
attack: one for renovation and one for destruction.
The difference between the prophet and the icono-
clast, it has been well said, is that the prophet always
knows the value of what he attacks. His onslaught
is made for the sake of that value. His quarrel with
the institution is not that it exists, and cumbers the
ground he wants to clear, but that it has failed of its
purpose, forgotten its function, and become something disastrously unlike its prime design and wholly

*An assemblage of such Catholic testimonies easily available to
readers of English is provided, with unexcelled scholarship and the highest impartiality, in Henry Charles Lea's great *History of the Inquisition
of the Middle Ages.*

unadapted to its purposed end. His attack is a challenge to it to be itself, to remember why it exists, to perform the work for which it was created.

Erasmus, and the little band of reformers who stood with him, were prophets in this as well as in other senses. In that day—before the rivalry of Protestantism had led to the sharpening of old dogmatic definitions and the forging of new ones; before Trent, before Jesuitism, before Jansenism and Gallicanism, before the Papal war of the XIX century against democracy, liberalism, and modern culture, which culminated in the probably irretrievable blunder of the Infallibility Decree of 1870—it was possible for a Catholic Christian to be, over large fields of speculation and action, a free thinker, and a critic and reformer of his Church. Erasmus could excoriate the rascally system of the monks, and denounce the abominations connected with the sale of indulgences, with a vigour unsurpassed by Luther himself. He could do this in books dedicated to liberal Popes and princes of the Church. He could bring to the attack all the incomparable resources of his learning, wit, irony, and descriptive skill. He could ridicule pilgrimages, fraudulent relics, the interpretation of natural events as miracles, the grotesque ignorance of secular and regular clergy alike, with as much freedom as any modern rationalist, and with far more point and effect. For he could do all this *without intending schism,* and without being misunderstood as wishing not the reformation but the destruction of the Church. In short, *he* could attack the Church like a modern patriot attacking corruption and misgovernment in his own country, under no suspicion of being a foreigner or a traitor, or of not loving that which he desires to amend. And every reader of his 'Colloquies,' his 'Adages,' his 'Notes on the New Testament,' and his 'Praise of Folly,'—to say nothing of his countless wonderful Letters,—knows with what inimitable wit and skill, with what unrivalled penetration and success, he did it.

§ III.

What Protestant, what rationalist, could have framed the indictment of Roman abuses more tellingly than Erasmus did, for example, in such comments as the following, taken from the Notes to his new translation (into Latin) of the New Testament?—

> Men are threatened or tempted into vows of celibacy. They can have license to go with harlots, but they must not marry wives. They may keep concubines and remain priests. If they take wives they are thrown to the flames. Parents who design their children for a celibate priesthood should emasculate them in their infancy, instead of forcing them, reluctant or ignorant, into a furnace of licentiousness.

Again, annotating the text (Matt. xxiii 27) about whited sepulchres:

> What would Jerome say, could he see the Virgin's milk exhibited for money, with as much honour paid to it as to the consecrated body of

Christ; the miraculous oil; the portions of the true
Cross, enough, if they were collected, to freight a
large ship? Here we have the hood of St. Francis,
there Our Lady's petticoat or St. Anne's comb, or
St. Thomas of Canterbury's shoes: presented not
as innocent aids to religion, but as the substance of
religion itself—and all through the avarice of
priests and the hypocrisy of monks playing on the
credulity of the people. Even bishops play their
parts in these fantastic shows, and approve and
dwell on them in their rescripts.

Once more, as to the moral character of the pre-
Reformation clergy, which is commonly believed to
have been maligned by Protestant slanderers. These
sentences, remember, are the work of a steady Catholic, contained in a book published with the approval
of a reforming Pope and some members of the Sacred
College at Rome:

Because in an age when priests were few and
widely scattered, St. Paul directed that no one
should be made a bishop who had been married a
second time, bishops, priests, and deacons are now
forbidden to marry at all. Other qualifications
are laid down by St. Paul as required for a
bishop's office, a long list of them. But not one
at present is held essential, except this one of
abstinence from marriage. *Homicide, parricide,
incest, piracy, sodomy, sacrilege,—these can be got
over, but marriage is fatal.* There are priests now
in vast numbers, enormous herds of them, seculars
and regulars, and it is notorious that very few of
them are chaste. The great proportion fall into
lust and incest, and open profligacy.

If any reader thinks it possible to doubt this rather

violent statement by Erasmus (though apparently nobody did in his own time), we might supplement it by the unconscious testimony of Sir Thomas More, who was not only a faithful son of the Roman Church, but by it is regarded as a martyr and has been beatified. Meeting Erasmus at Bruges when there on diplomatic business, More complained to him of the irksomeness of the long absence from home which such missions involved, and added, "Such an office does not suit us laymen; it is much fitter for you priests, who either have no wife and children at home, *or find them wherever you go."* The constant vehemence of Erasmus on this subject was doubtless due in part to the fact of his own illegitimate birth, which itself—if the legend be true —was due to the rigid refusal of the Church to permit marriage even to men in the minor orders. Erasmus was unquestionably illegitimate; but there is grave doubt of the truth of the pretty tale about his parents which is turned to such excellent account in Reade's great novel, 'The Cloister and the Hearth.'

Well, we have seen how Erasmus was feeling before the Lutheran storm had broken out. Let us listen to him a dozen years after the famous struggle over indulgences, when it was already becoming clear that the stubborn refusal of all reform had cloven Western Christendom in twain. This is from a letter to a friend under date of August 13th, 1529:

> What do they expect . . . who care nothing
> for Catholic piety, and care only to recover their
> old power and enjoyments? We were drunk or

asleep, and God has sent these stern schoolmasters to wake us up. The rope has been overstrained. It might have stood if they had slackened it a little, but they would rather have it break than save it by concession. The Pope is head of the Church, and as such deserves to be honoured. He stretched his authority too far, and so the first strand of the rope parted. Pardons and indulgences were tolerable within limits. Monks and commissaries filled the world with them to line their own pockets. In every church were the red boxes and the crosses and the Papal arms, *and the people were forced to buy.* So the second strand went. Then there was the invocation of saints. The images in churches at first served for ornaments and examples. By-and-by the walls were covered with scandalous pictures. The cult ran to idolatry; so parted a third. . . . What is more solemn than the Mass? But when stupid vagabond priests learn up two or three masses and repeat them over and over, as a cobbler makes shoes; when notorious profligates officiate at the Lord's table and the sacredest of mysteries is sold for money;—well, this strand is almost gone too. Secret confession may be useful; but when it is employed to extort money out of the terrors of fools, when an instrument designed as medicine for the soul is made an instrument of priestly villainy, this part of the cord will not last much longer either.

Priests who are loose in their lives, and yet demand to be honoured as superior beings, have brought their order into contempt. Careless of purity, careless what they do or how they live, the monks have trusted to their wealth and numbers to crush those whom they can no longer deceive. They pretended that their clothes would work miracles, that they could bring good luck into houses and keep the devil out. How is it at present? They used to be thought gods. They are now scarcely thought honest men.

I do not say that practices good in themselves should be condemned because they are abused. But I do say that we have ourselves given the occasion. We have no right to be surprised or angry, and we ought to consider quietly how best to meet the storm. As things go now there will be no improvement, let the dice fall which way they will. The Gospellers go for anarchy; the Catholics, instead of repenting of their sins, pile superstition on superstition; while Luther's disciples, if such they be, neglect prayers, neglect the fasts of the Church, and eat more on fast days than on common days. Papal constitutions, clerical privileges, are scorned and trampled on; and our wonderful champions of the Church do more than anyone to bring the Holy See into contempt.

Commenting on this letter, which he cites, Froude, in his Oxford Lectures on Erasmus, writes as follows: "Cardinal Newman said that Protestant tradition on the state of the Church before the Reformation is built on wholesale, unscrupulous lying. Erasmus was as true to the Holy See as Cardinal Newman himself. I do not know whether he is included among these unscrupulous liars. It is an easy way to get rid of an unpleasant witness." Froude might have added—though perhaps he thought it superfluous, because obvious—that in such letters to his contemporaries and fellow-Churchmen Erasmus invariably assumes their consent, as to matters of notorious and indisputable fact, to his pictures of the prevalent conditions.

§ IV.

Holding such convictions, why did not Erasmus go with the Lutheran movement? To answer this question aright is to penetrate to his secret, to grasp that view of the fundamental need of his time which made him the great man he was. Needless to say, like the other important men who had urged reform in the Church, yet declined to join the disruptive Protestants, he has had his reward in the hatred and abuse of the zealots of both sides. The monks of his own day declared that he was the cause of the whole disturbance. Luther's revolt was laid at his door, and a hundred pulpits rang with vituperation against him. He was a Lutheran: or, rather, Luther was an Erasmian. He had been Luther's teacher and inspirer. If now he refused to declare himself of the Lutheran party, it was only through cowardice. He had studied Greek, and urged others to study it. He had changed the text of the New Testament, instead of sticking to the good old Vulgate. Greek was the language of heresy. (So, within the past thirty years, in Italian seminaries, students have been warned not to study German, which now is the great language of heresy, as Greek was to the monkish ostriches of Erasmus' day.) His books reeked with impieties, blasphemies, mockeries of sacred things, et cœtera.

So declared his natural enemies, the monks. Of

course the charge was essentially false; but it was for them the only escape from admitting the truth, —which was that their own mountainous frauds, corruptions, superstitions, ignorances, extortions, and vices were the cause which had made some such movement as Luther's morally inevitable.

But what said Luther and his partisans? Reading the books of Erasmus, with an eye only to what they wanted to find, they not unnaturally thought that he was with them, and expected him to declare himself of their party. They were ready—nay, eager—to welcome him and accord to him the honoured position of leadership to which his learning, his genius, and his immense prestige entitled him. Their disappointment at his flat refusal to go with them was proportionate to the height and eagerness of their expectations from him. For them he was the traitor, the trimmer, the lost leader, who had abandoned what he knew to be the right cause, for 'a handful of silver' and 'a riband to stick in his coat.'

The misunderstanding was perhaps to have been expected; yet to considerate observers it is clear that Erasmus had done his utmost to avoid giving reasonable excuse for it. True, he agreed with much of Luther's criticism of current abuses—which, indeed, was little other than a paraphrase of what he had himself written; but he never for a moment desired to buy the correction of these abuses *at the cost of destroying the spiritual unity of Europe and enslaving the mind of the nations in the fetters*

INTRODUCTION

of a new dogmatism. Nothing, really, could be clearer than the warnings he gave Luther in the charming letter he wrote, in response to Luther's advances, in May, 1519. The following is the substance of it; and our especial attention is challenged by the passages I have italicized:

My dearest Brother in Christ,

Your letter, in which you show no less your truly Christian spirit than your great abilities, was extremely acceptable to me. I have no words to tell you what a sensation your writings have caused here [Louvain]. It is impossible to eradicate from people's minds *the utterly false suspicion that I have had a hand in them,* and that I am the ringleader of this 'faction,' as they call it.

Some thought an opportunity had been given them for extinguishing literature, for which they cherish the most deadly hatred, because they are afraid it will cloud the majesty of their divinity, which many of them prize before Christianity; and at the same time destroying myself, because they fancy I have some influence in promoting the cause of learning. The only weapons which they use are vociferation, rash assertion, tricks, detraction, and calumny; and had I not been present as a spectator—nay, had I not myself had experience of it—I should never have believed theologians could have gone to such extremes of madness. You would think it was a deadly contagion. . . . I have assured them that you were quite a stranger to me, that I have never read your books, and that I therefore neither sanction nor condemn anything you have said. I have only advised them not to bellow so fiercely in public before reading your books, but to leave the matter to those whose judgment ought to have the greatest weight; . . . but all to no purpose: such is the fury with which they carry on their ill-natured and calumnious disputes. How often have we agreed on terms of peace; how often have they, on the slightest suspicion, excited new disturbances! And these men, with such conduct as this, think themselves theologians. . .

These men have no hope of victory but in slander and deceit, and these are arts which I despise, because I rely on my own conscious rectitude. Towards you they are becoming somewhat milder; perhaps their own evil conscience leads them to fear the pens of the learned; and I would certainly paint them in their own colours, as they deserve, did not the teaching as well as the example of Christ dissuade me. Wild beasts may be tamed by kindness, but if you do good to these men it only makes them more ferocious. . . .

For myself, I am keeping such powers as I have to help the cause of the revival of letters. *And more, I think, is gained by politeness and moderation than by violence.* . . .

Instead of holding the universities in contempt, we ought rather to endeavour to recall them to more sober studies; and regarding opinions which are too generally received to be rooted all at once from people's minds, *it is better to reason upon them with close and convincing arguments than to deal in dogmatic assertions.* The violent wranglings in which some persons delight we can afford to despise, and it is useless attempting to answer them. *Let us be careful not to do or say anything savouring of arrogance and tending to encourage party feeling;* thus only, in my judgment, will our conduct be acceptable to the Spirit of Christ. Meantime, we must not permit our minds to be corrupted by anger, or hatred, *or vainglory; for this last is an insidious enemy, and especially dangerous in the cultivation of the religious feelings.* I do not, however, give you this advice because I think you need it, but in the hope that you will always go on as you have begun.

What could be kindlier or more considerate? Yet how could he, at that stage of events, have more plainly told Luther not to expect his co-operation in action destructive of the spiritual and cultural unity of the western world?

§ V.

But in forming our judgment on this misunderstanding of Erasmus by Luther and his followers, we must remember—what nowadays is seldom remembered either by Romanists or Protestants—that the cleavage of the Church, the setting up, as Seeley said, of two Christianities where before there was only one, was certainly at first not purposed or desired, or in the remotest degree anticipated, by Luther. It was not he who left the Church; it was the ecclesiastical authorities who drove him out. It was not his own will, but their obstinacy, that made him a sectary. He had, in full loyalty to the Pope, protested against a flagrant, monstrous, extortionate abuse, which in his innocence he had never dreamed could for a moment be sanctioned by the Head of the Church. He had pointed out that the indulgences were advertised by Tetzel as being something

which the Church had never authoritatively declared them to be, and as having powers which the
Church had never ascribed to them. Beyond any
possibility of question, Luther was right. from the
Roman point of view, in defining the authorized
meaning of an indulgence, and in protesting against
the pretences of Tetzel & Co., on the ground that
these were not only immoral and demoralizing, but
actually heretical from the theological standpoint.
An indulgence, as defined by theologians, was merely
the remittance of a penance or penalty imposed by
the Church. What the Church had imposed it could
remit,—as, nowadays, the State has power to cur-
tail or cancel a sentence judicially imposed upon a
lawbreaker. The indulgence was not a pardon for
sin. Only God could forgive sin. The priestly
shrift was, in theory, but declaratory of God's forgiveness; and this, at need, could be had as effica-
ciously without it. Forgiveness depended upon re-
pentance and amendment of life.

But the indulgences were, unquestionably, being
represented to the people as licenses to commit sin
without incurring the divine wrath or penalties.
As such they were described; as such they were
bought. Consequently, the money coming in from
them (for the building of St. Peter's at Rome) was
money obtained by false pretences; by the perver-
sion of the Christian religion as the Roman doctors
had themselves declared it. Remembering this, many
of us, when we stand under the dome of that vast,
impressive, pagan-like temple called St. Peter's in the

Eternal City, cannot resist the feeling that the irony of events has made it the very opposite of what it was designed to be. It was to have been the supreme symbol of the unity of Christendom; instead, it is its sepulchral monument;—itself the cause of the destruction of that unity which it was planned to represent and perpetuate.

It lies on the very face of Luther's famous XCV Theses that he was protesting as a Churchman, in the name and on behalf of the Pope, against an imposture which he confidently expected the Pope also to condemn and prohibit the moment he heard of it. Had the Pope done this,—had he and his advisers shown the slightest real insight into the situation,—the disaster of the schism might have been averted. The inevitable and long overdue reform, thus auspiciously begun, might have been gradually extended to the innumerable other perversions in the Church, against which the hurricane of lay wrath had for centuries been accumulating.

So thought Erasmus; or, rather, so he hoped. And, utterly as he refused to go with Luther when the blind perversity of Rome had made the breach impassable, he never ceased to insist, as we have seen, that the chief responsibility for the disruption lay with the Pope and his advisers.

§ VI.

What then are we to conclude regarding the charge of the Lutherans that Erasmus was a cowardly traitor to their cause? This:—that in his insight and foresight, his perception of the dynamics of history, his grasp of the development of the forces at work in society, Erasmus was a full three centuries ahead of them. as he was also of the official Church. Knowing fully the evils that clamoured for reform, he knew also that some remedies might be (and was convinced that Luther's remedy was) worse than the disease. He also knew——what the tribe of reformers are so reluctant to learn——that in human society there will always be evils to endure, and that the problem for statesmen often is to discern how much evil must be borne in order to secure some indispensable good: what is the least price that must be paid to prevent some enormous disaster.*

His was the balanced judgment that rises on the wings of wisdom and looks before and after; that can discern the remote development of tendencies at their beginning, and prognosticate the course of streams newly risen. And what he saw in the Lutheran method of reformation was the fatal sundering of the nexus that bound together the souls of men; the separation of nationalism from inter-

*'Am I to be treated as a criminal if I desire to see reforms carried out decently under constituted authority, instead of leaving them to violence and mob law? They speak of me as if they were trying to put a fire out, and I were interfering with them. *They would cure the diseases of a thousand years' standing with medicines which will be fatal to the whole body.*' (From a letter of Erasmus to a friend.) Again, from a letter to Melanchthon, December 10th, 1524: 'I would have had religion purified without destroying authority. License need not be given to sin. Practices grown corrupt by long usage might be gradually corrected without throwing everything into confusion. Luther sees certain things to be wrong, and in *flying blindly* at them causes more harm than he cures. *Order human things as you will, there will still be faults enough, and there are remedies worse than the disease.*'

nationalism,—whereas both are equally necessary
for human advancement; the multiplication of un-
verifiable dogmas about the unknowable,—whereas
the great need was for decreasing them, for abstain-
ing from presumptuous definitions of the indefin-
able, for leaving men free to think as their own
reason dictated on the riddles of philosophy and
theology, and getting them to extend their practice
of those ethical ideals which, for Erasmus, were the
substance of Christianity.

In brief, he was wiser than either of the contend-
ing factions. They were rival dogmatists, agreeing as
to the supremacy of dogma, differing only as to
which shibboleths should be held sacrosanct; he was
the anti-dogmatist, who wanted unity of spirit and
nobility of life far more than agreement in belief on
matters concerning which knowledge is impossible,
and the only certainty is that our best guesses are
utterly inadequate to the reality we strive to define.
Therefore he incurred the hatred of both. And to
this day his memory and reputation suffer from the
same causes. Although not officially disclaimed
nowadays by his own Church, yet his name is
scarcely ever mentioned, unless with condemnation,
by its writers and teachers. When such a liberal as
Lord Acton commends him, it is with the certainty
of official disapproval of his impartiality. In official eyes Erasmus stands, like Pascal, as an *enfant
terrible*. They cannot well repudiate one who, after
all, did champion the cause of Catholic unity against

the Lutheran separatists; yet they dare not encourage the reading of his works, since these at once blow sky-high the official myth, sedulously and laboriously constructed by the apologists, that there were no evils to reform in the Roman system; that Luther was a wilful schismatic; that the dissolution of the monasteries was due solely to the greed of lay princes and their favourites; and that the attacks on the character of monks, nuns, priests, and bishops are a set of slanders invented by the Protestant robbers to justify their crime in despoiling the Church of lands and goods dedicated to God.

This, I say, is the official myth. Read Erasmus, and you will see how altogether mythological it is. Had he been a Protestant, it would have been easy to call him a liar, and so discredit him with the faithful. Unluckily, he was a steady and unshakable Catholic; consequently that method is unavailing. Under the circumstances, the only resource was to prohibit the faithful from reading his works.*

*"After his works had been burned and banned by various Catholic countries, after he had been branded at the Council of Trent as a Pelagian and an impious heretic, his writings were officially prohibited by the Church, now in part, now altogether. The Spanish Inquisition first forbade the reading of 'Folly,' of the 'Epistles,' of the 'Paraphrases of the Gospels,' and of the 'Refutations of Luther,' and then proceeded, in the words of Milton, 'to rake through his entrails with a violation worse than the tomb,' publishing in the Expurgatorial Index of 1584, a list of passages to be deleted from his works on account of error, a list so long that it filled fifty-five quarto pages. But even this was found insufficient; the enumeration of his errors in the Expurgatorial Index of 1640 swelled to fifty-nine double-columned folio pages. Rome soon followed the lead of Spain. In 1559 Paul IV not only put Erasmus in the first class of forbidden authors, made up of those all of whose works were condemned, but added after his name: 'All his commentaries, notes, criticisms, colloquies, epistles, translations, books, and writings, even if they contain absolutely nothing against religion or about religion.' A Commission of the Council of Trent relaxed this censure slightly by pro-

INTRODUCTION

Among Protestants, his fame has suffered for the correspondent and complementary reasons. Romanists have disliked and distrusted him because of his candour about corruption and his insistence on reform. Protestants have disliked and distrusted him because to them he seemed insufficiently earnest about the corruptions he exposed, and unwilling to go their length to obtain reform. In a way, he has shared the fate of that extraordinary man, King Henry VIII of England, who also has been slandered, lied about, and utterly misunderstood by both schools of historians. Protestants hate and revile that monarch because he remained a Catholic, and would have none of their novel dogmas; Romanists detest and execrate him because he broke with the Pope, dissolved the monasteries, and made a successful claim for national self-determination,—in which he merely preceded by a few centuries the claim which almost all nations (including Italy itself) have since happily vindicated against the Papal assumptions.

I am far from thinking that the character and genius of King Henry were comparable with the character and genius of Erasmus. But it is worth while to remember that Erasmus, who knew him

hibiting the 'Colloquies,' the 'Folly,' the 'Tongue,' the 'Institution of Christian Marriage,' the Italian translation of the 'Paraphrase to Matthew,' and all other works on religion until expurgated by the Sorbonne. As this included the 'Adages,' there was little left, and in fact he was treated practically as an author of the first class."—Preserved Smith, *Erasmus* (1923).

It is my misfortune that I did not meet, until most of this introduction was already written, with Professor Smith's delightful volume, which is at once a credit to American scholarship and a boon to all lovers of Erasmus.

well, had a deep admiration for him in both aspects. In private letters, the sincerity of which it would be otiose to question, he repeatedly testifies to Henry's scholarship and fine taste, and betrays his conviction that the question of Henry's divorce from Catherine was a purely political one; for such divorces had repeatedly been granted by the Pope, and this one would have been, had the Pope been courageous enough to risk offending Charles V, or diplomatic enough to win Charles V's consent to it.

The blunt fact is that the Papacy lost Germany through refusing to make a timely and necessary concession to the lay conscience of the Germans, and threw away England through refusing to make a timely and necessary concession to the great political exigencies of the English. And, in the one case as in the other, the refusal had nothing to do with any moral or spiritual consideration, but was governed wholly by misconstrued expediencies of the most palpably secular and political character.

§ VII.

The Reformation, then, was inevitable, in the only sense in which that word ought ever to be applied to historical events. That is, there was no material or economic determinism about it; there never is about the religious, philosophical, cultural, and political developments of mankind. Economic tendencies and physical forces only *condition* human affairs; they do not determine them. They make change necessary; but only *some* change, never just the particular one that takes place. What the specific development shall be is decided by the mind and conscience that confronts the given situation, —the degree of insight and foresight, the amount of selfishness or unselfishness, the willingness to act for large and permanent objects, or the determination to concentrate on small, personal, or proximate goals. The course of European history during the previous four centuries had made it certain that some great change must come over the organization and expression of European religion in the XVI century. Had there been no Lutheran movement and no theological war, there would have been the movement for national autonomy, and the refusal any longer to send to Italian ecclesiastics revenues greater than those received by the national governments. But when Erasmus was meditating the 'Encomium Moriæ' and More conceiving the 'Utopia,' there still remained before the Western world a free choice as to what the change should be,—whether it should go the better and wiser way of Erasmus or the worse and less wise way of Luther. It went the worse way, not because it had to; not because men could not help it; but because the Pope and his advisers *would* not help it. With them—we must agree with Erasmus—the main responsibility lies. Luther was certainly driven into a schism which he did not at first intend. He was headstrong, sadly deficient in foresight, and had none of Erasmus' wonderful perception of the evil inherent in dogma. Yet we must not forget that to him also the world owes a great moral debt; and if it be true—as Luther's defenders maintain—that the Reformation could not have been secured by any other way than his, then we must admit that, terrific as was its cost to civilization, it was still so indispensably necessary that even at that cost it was worth while. Still, one cannot but share the sadness of Goethe that the intellectual progress of mankind should have been thrown back for centuries through the passions of the multitude being made the arbiters of questions which ought to have been decided by competent and humane thinkers.

Now, for the nobler as well as the baser nature, it is dangerous to come

> Between the pass and fell incensèd points
> Of mighty opposites.

And so it proved to Erasmus. He knew that the world needed a supernational organization, to testify that man is a spirit; that his destiny is prescribed by the inherent constitution of his spiritual nature; that life consists not in abundance of outward possessions, the life being more than meat and the body than raiment; that getting and spending, out of relation to the development of the personal and the social soul, is a laying waste of man's powers; that love is better than hate, peace than war, charity than greed, clean human love than animal lust, fraternal co-operation than murderous competition; and that the common spiritual nature which unites mankind is greater and deeper and more significant than the national, racial, physical, mental, psychical, and sexual characters that divide it. To witness to these truths, to promote the knowledge, understanding, love and practice of them, was the proper function of the Church Catholic. All its doctrines, sacraments, rituals, symbolisms, disciplines, organizations, were instrumental to this end. In so far as they made for it, they were commendable and useful. If in process of time they had become so overladen with dogma and superstition, and so corrupted by the exploitation of greedy, sensual, or class-minded priests and monks, that they no longer served their real purpose, they must be reformed and repristinated. Even though corrupted, the Church was indispensable,—in the sense of Voltaire's dictum about God, that if it had not existed it would have been necessary to invent it. It was the one organization that even professed to stand for the supremacy of the soul and of those things, spiritual and ethical, which pertain to the soul and contribute to its perfecting. Therefore its existence was all-important; and where it had become corrupt, its purgation, its drastic and thorough reformation, was no less all-important.

Thus Erasmus, with a prescience astounding in a man of his period, clearly perceived the altogether secondary place of dogma in the life of religion. He formulated a lovely definition of Christianity, as being 'nothing but true and perfect friendship, *dying with Christ and living in Christ';* a saying that might have been written by Jeremy Taylor or Matthew Arnold, and would have done honour to the greatest of the mystics. It proves that for him the life of religion was all, and dogma, by comparison, nothing. True, he picked no quarrel with such articles of belief as in his day were generally accepted and undisputed; he was quite ready to let sleeping dogmas lie; but, as we see in the ensuing pages, and by other of his writings, he wished that many of them had never been defined; for it is the defined dogma that makes the heresy and the heretic. When a man holds Christianity to consist in dying and living with Christ—that is, renouncing and subduing, as Christ renounced and subdued, his lower nature, thereby releasing into full and free life his true, high, distinctive, spiritual selfhood—he must needs grow somewhat impatient of a mass of definitions concerning Christ's nature and antecedents, framed upon guesswork data by men with a turn for metaphysical speculation, but—as the history of the Council of Nicæa and other dogma-fabricators shows only too clearly—with no turn at all for 'dying with Christ and living in him' in the sense of Erasmus and St. Paul. Consider the many scorching and contemptuous satires Erasmus wrote about the Scotists, the ridicule he poured upon their definitions and distinctions.* His strong sense of

---

*One of the best of these occurs in a letter to his friend Thomas Grey, dated 1499, but possibly written earlier (the dating of all Erasmus' letters being very uncertain). He tells the old story of Epimenides the Cretan, who was said to have slept for forty-seven years, and continues thus:

'But come, dear Thomas, what think you Epimenides was dreaming of for so many years? What else but those most subtle subtleties of which the Scotists are now so proud? For that Epimenides has come to life again in Scotus I should not hesitate to swear. What if you should

the absurdity of venturing thus with confident foot into regions unknown and unexplorable, shows us how resentful he was even of much defined dogma, and explains his intense determination to resist what he saw must come—namely, the fabrication of a whole new system of dogmas by the Lutherans, and, as an inevitable counter-stroke to that, the piling of new credal burdens upon men's minds by the Papists.

§ VIII.

One of the thoughts that haunted Erasmus all his life, and that should do much to bespeak for him the attention of men today, was his profound and noble detestation of war.   What he has to say on this in the 'Praise of Folly,' the reader can easily see by turning to page 164 of this book.   But that this was no passing thought with him is shown by many

see Erasmus sitting κεχηνότα (with mouth open) among those holy Scotists, while Gryllardus delivers a prelection from a lofty chair? If you should see his brow contracted, his eyes fixed, his face full of anxious thought?   You would say he was another man.   They say that the mysteries of this learning cannot be understood by one who has any commerce whatever with the Muses or with the Graces.   If you have acquired any knowledge of polite literature you must unlearn it; if you have drunk from the waters of Helicon you must spew them up again.   I am doing my utmost not to say anything in pure Latin, to abandon all grace and wit, and I think I am succeeding; there is hope that they will at length acknowledge Erasmus.   But to what purpose is all this, you will say?   That you may not hereafter expect anything from Erasmus that savours of his old studies or habits, remembering among whom I live, among whom I sit every day: so look out for another playmate.   But, lest you mistake me, most sweet Grey, I would not have you interpret these things as said against theology, for which, as you know, I have always entertained the greatest respect: I only wished to have a joke at the expense of certain theologists of the present generation, whose brains are rotten, their language barbarous, their apprehension dull, their learning thorny, their manners rude, *their life a mere scene of hypocrisy, and their hearts as black as hell.'*

of his other writings, particularly by repeated state-
ments in his correspondence. The following is a
characteristic outburst, taken from a letter to the
Abbot of St. Bertin, written in 1513 or 1514:

> . . . I see great disturbances likely to arise,
> the issue of which it is impossible to predict. Oh,
> that God would be merciful and still this storm
> which is raging in the Christian world! I often
> wonder what it is that urges, I will not say
> Christians, but men, to such a pitch of madness
> that they will make every effort, incur any ex-
> pense, and meet the greatest dangers, for their
> mutual destruction. For what else are we doing
> all our lives but waging war? We are worse than
> the dumb animals, for among them it is only the
> wild beasts that wage war, and even they do not
> fight among themselves, but with beasts of a
> different species, and that with the weapons
> with which nature has furnished them; not as
> we do, with machines invented by the art of the
> devil, nor for all manner of causes, but either
> in defence of their young or for food. Can we,
> who glory in the name of Christ, whose pre-
> cepts and example taught us only gentleness, we
> who are members of one body, who are one flesh,
> and grow by the same spirit, who are nourished
> by the same sacraments, attached to the same head,
> and called to the same immortality, and who hope
> for the highest communion, that, as Christ and the
> Father are one, so we also may be one in Him,—
> can we, I say, think of anything in this world of
> such value that it should provoke us to war?—a
> thing so ruinous, so hateful, that even when it is
> most just, no truly good man can approve of it.
> Pray consider by whom it is carried on,—by

homicides, gamblers, scoundrels of every kind, by the lowest class of hirelings, who care more for a little gain than for their lives.*   It is such as these that make the best soldiers, since they only do for pay and for glory what they did before at their own risk.   These offscourings of mankind must be received into your fields, into your cities, to enable you to carry on war.   In short, we must put ourselves at the mercy of these men, while we desire to revenge ourselves on some one else.   Add to this the crimes which are committed under the pretext of war, since 'amid the din of arms good laws are silent,'—how many robberies, sacrileges, rapes, and other disgraceful deeds such as one is ashamed even to mention.   This corruption of morals must needs last for many years, even after the war is over.   Then think of the expense, so that, even if you conquer, you still lose far more than you gain;—what kingdom, indeed, could you put against the life and blood of so many thousand human beings?

§ IX.

The 'Praise of Folly' belongs to the year 1509 or 1510.   (It seems to have been first printed in 1511, though there is some possibility that a mutilated and unauthorized edition may have appeared earlier.) Thus it goes back to the days before the Lutheran storm; to the years of Erasmus' closest connection

*This, of course, refers to the practice almost universal in the XVI century, of employing hired professional soldiers of any nationality. There were multitudes of these ready to fight at any time. in any quarrel, and on any side that would pay them and give them the chance of loot. One cannot say that the horrors of war have been materially reduced by the abolition of this system; but I suppose it is less outrageous to refined feelings to have our atrocities committed for us only by patriots fighting for their own country.

with England, when his dear friends Colet, War-
ham, Fisher, and More were giving to religion a renewed inwardness, to learning an immense impetus,
and to the rebuking of scandal in the Church a
steady censure—sometimes grave, sometimes satirical
—which promised the kind of reform Erasmus so
ardently desired. It has the buoyancy of youth still
about it. It breathes the freshness of hope and the
gaiety of confidence in the future. As a satire, it
has little even of the implicit gloom of the 'Utopia,'
and nothing of the deadly cynicism of 'Gulliver.' It
is the outpouring of joy, not of tortured despair.
What fools these mortals be,—yet what potency of
amendment is in them!

The future still looks bright to Erasmus. It is
the day of the young men. The brilliant Prince
Henry has just ascended the English throne, and it
will be many a day before he shall falsify the great
hopes he has already awakened in hosts of discerning
men, besides More and Erasmus. Prince Charles,
destined within a few years to assume the succession
to nineteen kingdoms and principalities, is already
on the horizon, as is also the knightly and gallant
lad who ere long shall be Francis I of France. All
are well taught, all in sympathy with the New
Learning, and ready to abet Erasmus in his cam-
paign against stupidity and obscurantism. These
stars of promise are destined to sink among the
blood-red clouds of a grim morrow; but as yet the
promise is radiant, its falsification indiscernible.

There is a new stir in the souls of men. Columbus and his followers have placed America on the map, and the Portuguese explorers are filling in the outlines of Africa. The spirit of Greece is reviving with its language, and the Renaissance has found in the art of printing its mightiest instrument and opportunity. The lay conscience of Europe is in full revolt against the shams, absurdities, and ignorances of monkery. How otherwise could the daring rebukes of Erasmus have won such universal applause, and have been in such demand as to call for edition after edition?* When Leo X was Pope,—Leo X, who chuckled over the 'Praise of Folly' and remarked, 'Here is our old friend again'!—and a son of the New Birth like Henry VIII king of England, it may well have seemed to Erasmus, sensitive as he ever was to the rustling of the Time-Spirit's wings, that

> The world's great age began anew,
> The golden years returned.

He was sustained amid his poverty (a poverty due rather to carelessness in expenditure than to paucity of income, at least in his riper years) by the discriminating applause of the masters of scholarship and of the princes, ecclesiastical and secular. True, the obscurantists hated him and would have liked to tear him limb from limb, but his standing was so secure that he could afford to laugh them to scorn. Europe was at his feet. He enjoyed, and was long to enjoy, a literary dictatorship as universal as it was beneficent.

*No less than forty editions of the 'Folly' appeared during the lifetime of Erasmus. There have been countless translations.

IN PRAISE OF ERASMUS

One of the conditions of his supremacy in the world of letters was his remarkable mastery of what was then the universal language of literature, scholarship, diplomacy, and international intercourse. Latin, in which all the writing of Erasmus was done, was at that time a far more living thing than it has ever been since. We find Erasmus, a born Dutchman, writing to a Dutch correspondent in Latin, and apologising for doing so on the ground of his imperfect acquaintance with his own native tongue. There are evidences that by sojourning in France and England, he had scraped up a little speaking knowledge of the languages of those countries, and he must have been familiar with Italian, though he disliked it. Latin was the language that he had studied till he knew it upside down and inside out; and, as a thorough-going internationalist, he probably looked with distrust, if not contempt, on the tendency, which in his time was still only at its beginning, to use the national vernaculars as media of literary expression.

It is the way of the world never to be willing to have two good things at once. National languages and literatures are excellent things; and everybody would agree that if we had to choose between them and an international language and literature, we should have to vote for the former and against the latter. That, in fact, is what the world has done. But it is, in a way, a misfortune that of these two good things mankind could not have chosen both. Such great examples as Dante, and among our own

INTRODUCTION

race Bacon and Milton, may remind us that it is
perfectly possible for men to be literary masters in
two languages, one national and one international.
Erasmus at once had the ear of the entire educated
public of Europe for every book he wrote, and he
could travel over the Continent and into England
with the certainty of being able to enter freely into
conversation with the society he met at every uni-
versity, at almost every Court, and in the majority
of gentlemen's houses. The mere obstacle of language would make it impossible nowadays, even for
an Erasmus, to enjoy the instantaneous access to the
general mind which rendered possible his literary
dictatorship. We talk much today of our inter-
nationalism, and are increasingly feeling the need
of a universally intelligible medium of intercourse.
The absence of such an instrument makes us all
provincial, as compared with the contemporaries of
Erasmus. A man today would need half a dozen
languages before he could command even the social
entrée that Erasmus enjoyed. And, inasmuch as no
man can be a master of literary style in half a dozen
languages, no man can (unless interest in his writing
is excited by something other than its own appeal,
so that he is at once translated) achieve in his own
time the fame and influence of our old master. One
may hope that the increasing need for an international language will lead, during this century, to the
adoption of such an instrument. There is no great
practical difficulty in the way. The revival of Latin
for the purpose is probably neither possible nor de-

sirable, but Dr. Zamenhof long since proved that the 'Esperanto,' which he so ingeniously concocted, has all the flexibility and adaptability of a naturally evolved language. Inasmuch as anybody can learn to write and speak it intelligibly in a week, it is evident that nothing but prejudice and stupidity, or that excessive provincial-mindedness which afflicts all nations today, stands between the world and this great convenience.

We may fairly assume, then, that the look and feel of his world were pleasant and hopeful enough when Erasmus, on his horse's back, was stringing together in his mind the argument and the jokes which he afterwards dashed off in the 'Encomium Moriæ.' He was an amazingly rapid worker, and there is nothing incredible in the tradition that the immortal skit was written in a week.

§ X.

I like to think that that living and radiant portrait by Holbein shows him as he looked when penning this glorious 'roast' of all the follies and humbugs of his age. One divines, behind those veiling lids, eyes luminous with fun and satire, with insight into the absurdities of mankind, yet with love for mankind in spite of them. Look at the delicate, mobile, twitching lips, electric with subtlety and humour. Look at the noble head, a living temple of mastered learning fused to wisdom. It is no ascetic's face, yet the severity of its chiselling bespeaks a discipline far sterner than the ascetic's.

INTRODUCTION

Here is a man to whom truth is a passion, learning an enthusiasm, reformation a crusade; yet to whom tolerance is compulsive, catholicity an achieved virtue, and the method and secret of Jesus are living realities, experimentally verified: the fine flower of the Renaissance, the exquisite blending of Hellenism with Hebraism.

Humanist, anti-dogmatist, war-hater, internationalist, lover of fine letters; humourist, satirist, Christian freethinker; smiter of humbugs, roaster of shams; vivid depicter of a life that in its externals has changed, but in its essentials is unchanging; lover of humanity; seer of a noble vision of unity in diversity, which the world to its loss and sorrow passed by; prophet, thus, of an ideal to which in changed form we must return—and which indeed we already are, at Geneva and elsewhere, tentatively seeking to re-embody: such was Erasmus, the first of the moderns.

To know him is to love him. May the reading of this edition of the 'Praise of Folly' lead many to his other works and to the story of his life. One could wish them no greater joy and privilege.

HORACE J. BRIDGES.

Chicago, September 25, 1924.

IN PRAISE OF ERASMUS

NOTE.—*The ensuing translation was made in 1683 by an Oxford undergraduate, WHITE KEN-NETT, afterwards Bishop of Peterborough. I have compared it with the Latin, and made some few changes in the interest of accuracy, but have inter-fered as little as possible with KENNETT'S quaint and racy English. The few notes I have added speak for themselves.*

Readers who are making their first acquaintance with ERASMUS in these pages, and who wish to extend it, are advised to proceed next to his 'Collo-quies'; to Professor PRESERVED SMITH'S admirable volume, already cited; to FROUDE'S fascinating Ox-ford lectures on 'The Life and Letters of Erasmus'; to ROBERT BLACKLEY DRUMMOND'S 'Erasmus: His Life and Character'; to FREDERIC SEEBOHM'S 'Ox-ford Reformers' (Erasmus, Colet, More); and to P. S. ALLEN'S 'The Age of Erasmus.'

H. J. B.

The return of the prodigal son

EPISTLE TO
SIR THOMAS MORE

IN MY LATE TRAVELS from Italy into England, that I might not trifle away my time in the rehearsal of old wives' fables, I thought it more pertinent to employ my thoughts in reflecting upon some past studies, or calling to remembrance several of those highly learned, as well as smartly ingenious, friends I had here left behind, among whom you (dear SIR) were represented as the chief; whose memory, while absent at this distance, I respect with no less a complacency than I was wont while present to enjoy your more intimate conversation, which last afforded me the greatest satisfaction I could possibly hope for. Having therefore resolved to be a doing, and deeming that time improper for any serious concerns, I thought good to divert myself with drawing up a panegyrick upon Folly. How! what maggot (say you) put this in your head? Why, the first hint, Sir, was your own surname of More, which comes as near the literal sound of the word* as you yourself are distant from the signification of it; and that in all men's judgments is vastly wide. In the next place, I supposed that this kind of sporting wit would be by you more especially accepted of—by

* Μωρία.

you, Sir, that are wont with this sort of jocose
raillery (such as, if I mistake not, is neither dull nor
impertinent) to be mightily pleased, and in your
ordinary converse to approve yourself a Democritus
junior: for truly, as you do from a singular vein
of wit very much dissent from the common herd of
mankind; so, by an incredible affability and pliable-
ness of temper, you have the art of suiting your
humour with all sorts of companies. I hope therefore you will not only readily accept of this rude
essay as a token from your friend, but take it under
your more immediate protection, as being dedicated
to you, and by that title adopted for yours, rather
than to be fathered as my own. And it is a chance if
there be wanting some quarrelsome persons that
will shew their teeth, and pretend these fooleries are
either too buffoon-like for a grave divine, or too
satyrical for a meek Christian, and so will exclaim
against me as if I were vamping up some old farce,
or acted anew the Lucian again with a peevish snarl-
ing at all things. But those who are offended at the
lightness and pedantry of this subject, I would have
them consider that I do not set myself for the first
example of this kind, but that the same has been
oft done by many considerable authors. For thus,
several ages since, Homer wrote of no more weighty
a subject than of a war between the frogs and
mice, Virgil of a gnat and a pudding-cake, and
Ovid of a nut. Polycrates commended the cruelty
of Busiris; and Isocrates, that corrects him for this,
did as much for the injustice of Glaucus. Favorinus

extolled Thersites, and wrote in praise of a quartan ague. Synesius pleaded in behalf of baldness; and Lucian defended a sipping fly. Seneca drollingly related the deifying of Claudius; Plutarch the dialogue betwixt Gryllus and Ulysses; Lucian and Apuleius the story of an ass; and a certain Grunnius Corocotta records the last will of a hog, of which St. Hierom* makes mention. So that if they please, let themselves think the worst of me, and fancy to themselves that I was all this while a playing at pushpin, or riding astride on a hobby-horse. For how unjust is it, if when we allow different recreations to each particular course of life, we afford no diversion to studies; especially when trifles may be a whet to more serious thoughts, and comical matters may be so treated of, as that a reader of ordinary sense may possibly thence reap more advantage than from some more big and stately argument: as while one in a long-winded oration descants in commendation of rhetoric or philosophy, another in a fulsome harangue sets forth the praise of his nation, a third makes a zealous invitation to a holy war with the Turks, another confidently sets up for a fortune-teller, and a fifth states questions upon mere impertinences. But as nothing is more childish than to handle a serious subject in a loose, wanton style, so is there nothing more pleasant than so to treat of trifles, as to make them seem nothing less than what their name imports. As to what relates to myself, I must be forced to submit to the judgment of

*Jerome.

others; yet, except I am too partial to judge in my own case, I am apt to believe I have praised Folly in such a manner as not to have deserved the name of fool for my pains. To reply now to the objection of satyricalness, wits have been always allowed this privilege, that they might be smart upon any transactions of life, if so be their liberty did not extend to railing; which makes me wonder at the tendereared humour of this age, which will admit of no address without the prefatory repetition of all formal titles: nay, you may find some so preposterously devout, that they will sooner wink at the greatest affront against our Saviour, than be content that a prince, or a pope, should be nettled with the least joke or gird, especially in what relates to their ordinary customs. But he who so blames men's irregularities as to lash at no one particular person by name, does he (I say) seem to carp so properly as to teach and instruct? And if so, how am I concerned to make any farther excuse? Beside, he who in his strictures points indifferently at all, he seems not angry at one man, but at all vices.

Therefore, if any singly complain they are particularly reflected upon, they do but betray their own guilt, at least their cowardice. Saint Hierom dealt in the same argument at a much freer and sharper rate; nay, and he did not sometimes refrain from naming the persons: whereas I have not only stifled the mentioning any one person, but have so tempered my style, as the ingenious reader will easily perceive I aimed at diversion rather than satire. Neither did

TO SIR THOMAS MORE

I so far imitate Juvenal, as to rake into the sink of vices to procure a laugh, rather than create a hearty abhorrence. If there be any one that after all remains yet unsatisfied, let him at least consider that there may be good use made of being reprehended by Folly, which since we have feigned as speaking, we must keep up that character which is suitable to the person introduced.

But why do I trouble you, Sir, with this needless apology: you, that are so peculiar a patron as, though the cause itself be none of the best, you can at least give it the best protection. Farewell.

Ex rure. Quinto Idus Junias, Anno MDVIII.

The return of the prodigal daughter

IN PRAISE OF
FOLLY

An oration, of feigned matter, spoken by FOLLY
in her own person.

HOW SLIGHTLY SOEVER I am esteemed
in the common vogue of the world (for
I well know how disingenuously Folly is
decried, even by those who are themselves the greatest fools), yet it is from my influence alone that the
whole universe receives her ferment of mirth and
jollity; of which this may be urged as a convincing
argument, in that as soon as I appeared to speak before this numerous assembly all their countenances
were gilded over with a lively sparkling pleasant-
ness: you soon welcomed me with so encouraging
a look, you spurred me on with so cheerful a hum,
that truly in all appearance, you seem now flushed
with a good dose of reviving nectar, when as just
before you sate drowsy and melancholy, as if you
were lately come out of some hermit's cell. But
as it is usual, that as soon as the sun peeps from her
eastern bed, and draws back the curtains of the
darksome night; or as when, after a hard winter,
the restorative spring breathes a more enlivening
air, nature forthwith changes her apparel, and all
things seem to renew their age; so at the first

sight of me you all unmask, and appear in more lively colours. That therefore which expert orators can scarce effect by all their little artifice of eloquence, to wit, a raising the attentions of their auditors to a composedness of thought, this a bare look from me has commanded. The reason why I appear in this odd kind of garb, you shall soon be informed of, if for so short a while you will have but the patience to lend me an ear; yet not such a one as you are wont to hearken with to your reverend preachers, but as you listen withal to mountebanks, buffoons, and merry-andrews; in short, such as formerly were fastened to Midas, as a punishment for his affront to the god Pan. For I am now in a humour to act awhile the sophist: yet not of that sort who undertake the drudgery of tyrannizing over schoolboys, and teach a more than womanish knack of brawling; but in imitation of those ancient ones, who to avoid the scandalous epithet of wise, preferred this title of sophists: the task of these was to celebrate the worth of gods and heroes. Prepare therefore to be entertained with a panegyrick, yet not upon Hercules, Solon, or any other grandee, but on myself, that is, upon Folly.

And here I value not their censure that pretend it is foppish and affected for any person to praise himself: yet let it be as silly as they please, if they will but allow it needful: and indeed what is more befitting than that Folly should be the trumpet of her own praise, and dance after her own pipe? for who can set me forth better than myself? or who

Folly entertains

can pretend to be so well acquainted with my condition?

And yet farther, I may safely urge, that all this is no more than the same with what is done by several seemingly great and wise men, who with a new-fashioned modesty employ some paltry orator or scribbling poet, whom they bribe to flatter them with some high-flown character, that shall consist of mere lies and shams; and yet the persons thus extolled shall bristle up, and, peacock-like, bespread their plumes, while the impudent parasite magnifies the poor wretch to the skies, and proposes him as a complete pattern of all virtues, from each of which he is yet as far distant as heaven itself from hell: what is all this in the mean while, but the tricking up a daw in stolen feathers; a labouring to change the blackamoor's hue, and the drawing on a pigmy's frock over the shoulders of a giant?

Lastly, I verify the old observation, that allows him a right of praising himself, who has nobody else to do it for him: for really, I cannot but admire at that ingratitude, shall I term it, or blockishness of mankind, who when they all willingly pay to me their utmost devoir, and freely acknowledge their respective obligations: that notwithstanding this, there should have been none so grateful or complaisant as to have bestowed upon me a commendatory oration, especially when there have not been wanting such as at a great expense of sweat, and loss of sleep, have in elaborate speeches given high encomiums to tyrants, agues, flies, baldness, and such like trumperies.

I shall entertain you with a hasty and unpremeditated, but so much the more natural discourse. My venting it *ex tempore,* I would not have you think proceeds from any principles of vain glory by which ordinary orators square their attempts, who (as it is easy to observe) when they are delivered of a speech that has been thirty years a conceiving, nay, perhaps at last, none of their own, yet they will swear they wrote it in a great hurry, and upon very short warning: whereas the reason of my not being provided beforehand is only because it was always my humour constantly to speak that which lies uppermost. Next, let no one be so fond as to imagine, that I should so far stint my invention to the method of other pleaders, as first to define, and then divide my subject, *i.e.,* myself. For it is equally hazardous to attempt the crowding her within the narrow limits of a definition, whose nature is of so diffusive an extent, or to mangle and disjoin that, to the adoration whereof all nations unitedly concur. Beside, to what purpose is it to lay down a definition for a faint resemblance, and mere shadow of me, while appearing here personally, you may view me at a more certain light? And if your eye-sight fail not, you may at first blush discern me to be her whom the Greeks term Μωρία, the Latins *Stultitia.*

But why need I have been so impertinent as to have told you this, as if my very looks did not

sufficiently betray what I am; or supposing any be
so credulous as to take me for some sage matron or
goddess of wisdom, as if a single glance from me
would not immediately correct their mistake, while
my visage, the exact reflex of my soul, would supply
and supersede the trouble of any other confessions:
for I appear always in my natural colours and an
unartificial dress, and never let my face pretend one
thing, and my heart conceal another; nay, and in
all things I am so true to my principles, that I cannot be so much as counterfeited, even by those who
challenge the name of wits, yet indeed are no better
than jackanapes tricked up in gaudy clothes, and
asses strutting in lions' skins; and how cunningly
soever they carry it, their long ears appear, and betray what they are.   These in troth are very rude
and disingenuous, for while they apparently belong
to my party, yet among the vulgar they are so
ashamed of my relation, as to cast it in others' dish
for a shame and reproach: wherefore since they are
so eager to be accounted wise, when in truth they
are extremely silly, what, if to give them their due,
I dub them with the title of wise fools: and herein
they copy after the example of some modern orators,
who swell to that proportion of conceitedness, as to
vaunt themselves for so many giants of eloquence,
if with a double-tongued fluency they can plead
indifferently for either side, and deem it a very
doughty exploit if they can but interlard a Latin
sentence with some Greek word, which for seeming
garnish they crowd in at a venture; and rather than

be at a stand for some cramp words, they will furnish up a long scroll of old obsolete terms out of
some musty author, and foist them in, to amuse
the reader with, that those who understand them
may be tickled with the happiness of being acquainted with them: and those who understand
them not, the less they know the more they may
admire; whereas it has been always a custom to
those of our side to contemn and undervalue whatever is strange and unusual, while those that are
better conceited of themselves will nod and smile,
and prick up their ears, that they may be thought
easily to apprehend that, of which perhaps they do
not understand one word.   And so much for this.
Pardon the digression; now I return.

Of my name I have informed you, Sirs; what
additional epithet to give you I know not, except
you will be content with that of Most Foolish; for
under what more proper appellation can the goddess
Folly greet her devotees?   But since there are few
acquainted with my family and original, I will now
give you some account of my extraction.

First then, my father was neither the Chaos, nor
Orcus,* nor Saturn, nor Jupiter, nor any of those
old, worn-out, grandsire gods, but Plutus, the very
same that, maugre Homer, Hesiod, nay, in spite of
Jove himself, was the primary father of the universe;
at whose alone beck, for all ages, religion and civil
policy have been successively undermined and re-
established; by whose powerful influence war, peace,

*The god of hell.

empire, debates, justice, magistracy, marriage, leagues, compacts, laws, arts, (I have almost run myself out of breath, but) in a word, all affairs of Church and State, and business of private concern, are severally ordered and administered; without whose assistance all the Poets' gang of deities, nay, I may be so bold as to say the very majordomos of heaven, would either dwindle into nothing, or at least be confined to their respective homes without any ceremonies of devotional address: whoever he combats with as an enemy, nothing can be armour-proof against his assaults; and whosoever he sides with as a friend, may grapple at even hand with Jove, and all his bolts. Of such a father I may well brag; and he begot me, not of his brain, as Jupiter did the hag Pallas, but of a pretty young nymph, famed for wit no less than beauty: and this feat was not done amidst the embraces of dull nauseous wedlock, but what gave a greater gust to the pleasure, it was done at a stolen bout, as we may modestly phrase it. But to prevent your mistaking me, I would have you understand that my father was not that Plutus in Aristophanes, old, dry, withered, sapless and blind; but the same in his younger and brisker days, and when his veins were more impregnated, and the heat of his youth somewhat higher inflamed by a chirping cup of nectar, which for a whet to his lust he had just before drank very freely of at a merry-meeting of the gods. And now presuming you may be inquisitive after my birth-place (the quality of the place we are born in, being

now looked upon as a main ingredient of gentility),
I was born neither in the wandering Delos, nor on
the frothy sea, nor in any of these privacies, where
too forward mothers are wont to retire for an un-
discovered delivery; but in the Fortunate Islands,
where all things grow without the toil of husbandry,
wherein there is no drudgery, no distempers, no old
age, where in the fields grow no daffodills, mallows,
onions, pease, beans, or such kind of trash, but there
give equal divertisement to our sight and smelling,
rue, all-heal, bugloss, marjoram, herb of life, roses,
violets, hyacinth, and such like fragrances as per-
fume the gardens of Adonis.   And being born
amongst these delights I did not, like other infants,
come crying into the world, but perked up, and
laughed immediately in my mother's face.   And
there is no reason I should envy Jove for having a
she-goat to his nurse, since I was more creditably
suckled by two jolly nymphs; the name of the first
Drunkenness, one of Bacchus's offspring, the other
Ignorance, the daughter of Pan; both which you
may here behold among several others of my train
and attendants, whose particular names, if you
would fain know, I will give you in short.   This,
who goes with a mincing gait, and holds up her
head so high, is Self-Love.   She that looks so spruce,
and makes such a noise and bustle, is Flattery.
That other, which sits mumchance, as if she were half
asleep, is called Forgetfulness.   She that leans on
her elbow, and sometimes yawningly stretches out
her arms, is Laziness.   This, that wears a plighted

Proud peacocks

garland of flowers, and smells so perfumed, is Pleasure. The other, which appears in so smooth a skin, and pampered-up flesh, is Sensuality. She that stares so wildly, and rolls about her eyes, is Madness. As to those two gods whom you see playing among the lasses, the name of the one is Intemperance, the other Sound Sleep. By the help and service of this retinue I bring all things under the verge of my power, lording it over the greatest kings and potentates.

You have now heard of my descent, my education, and my attendance; that I may not be taxed as presumptuous in borrowing the title of a goddess, I come now in the next place to acquaint you what obliging favours I everywhere bestow, and how largely my jurisdiction extends: for if, as one has ingenuously noted, to be a god is no other than to be a benefactor to mankind; and if they have been thought deservedly deified who have invented the use of wine, corn, or any other convenience for the well-being of mortals, why may not I justly bear the van among the whole troop of gods, who in all, and toward all, exert an unparalleled bounty and beneficence?

For instance, in the first place, what can be more dear and precious than life itself? and yet for this are none beholden, save to me alone. For it is neither the spear of throughly-begotten Pallas, nor the buckler of cloud-gathering Jove, that multiplies and propagates mankind: but that prime father of the universe, who at a displeasing nod makes heaven

itself to tremble, he (I say) must lay aside his frightful ensigns of majesty, and put away that grim
aspect wherewith he makes the other gods to quake,
and, stage player-like, must lay aside his usual character, if he would do that, the doing whereof he
cannot refrain from, *i.e.,* getting of children.   The
next place to the gods is challenged by the Stoicks;
but give me one as stoical as ill-nature can make
him, and if I do not prevail on him to part with his
beard, that bush of wisdom (though no other ornament than what nature in more ample manner has
given to goats), yet at least he shall lay by his gravity, smooth up his brow, relinquish his rigid tenets,
and in despite of prejudice become sensible of some
passion in wanton sport and dallying.   In a word,
this dictator of wisdom shall be glad to take Folly
for his diversion, if ever he would arrive to the
honour of a father.   And why should I not tell my
story out?   To proceed then: is it the head, the face,
the breasts, the hands, the ears, or other more comely
parts, that serve for instruments of generation?   I
trow not, but it is that member of our body which
is so odd and uncouth as can scarce be mentioned
without a smile.   This part, I say, is that fountain
of life, from which originally spring all things in a
truer sense than from the Pythagorean fount. Add to
this, what man would be so silly as to run his head
into the collar of a matrimonial noose, if (as wise
men are wont to do) he had beforehand duly con-
sidered the inconveniences of a wedded life?   Or
indeed what woman would open her arms to receive

The marriage vow

the embraces of a husband, if she did but forecast
the pangs of child-birth, and the plague of being
a nurse? Since then you owe your birth to the
bride-bed, and (what was preparatory to that) the
solemnizing of marriage to my waiting-woman
Madness, you cannot but acknowledge how much
you are indebted to me. Beside, those who had once
dearly bought the experience of their folly, would
never re-engage themselves in the same entanglement by a second match, if it were not occasioned
by the forgetfulness of past dangers. And Venus
herself (whatever Lucretius pretends to the contrary) cannot deny, but that without my assistance,
her procreative power would prove weak and ineffectual. It was from my sportive and tickling
recreation that proceeded the old crabbed philosophers, and those who now supply their stead, the
mortified monks and friars; as also kings, priests,
and popes, nay, the whole tribe of poetic gods, who
are at last grown so numerous, as in the camp of
heaven (though ne'er so spacious), to jostle for elbow room.

But it is not sufficient to have made it appear
that I am the source and original of all life, except
I likewise shew that all the benefits of life are equally
at my disposal. And what are such? Why, can
any one be said properly to live to whom pleasure
is denied? You will give me your assent; for there
is none I know among you so wise, shall I say, or
so silly, as to be of a contrary opinion. The Stoics
indeed contemn, and pretend to banish pleasure, but

this is only a dissembling trick, and a putting the vulgar out of conceit with it, that they may more quietly engross it to themselves: but I dare them now to confess what one stage of life is not melancholy, dull, tiresome, tedious, and uneasy, unless we spice it with pleasure, that condiment of Folly. Of the truth whereof the never enough to be commended Sophocles is sufficient authority, who gives me the highest character in that sentence of his, *In nihil sapiendo vita iucundissima*: 'To know nothing is the sweetest life.'

Yet abating from this, let us examine the case more narrowly. Who knows not that the first scene of infancy is far the most pleasant and delightsome? What then is it in children that makes us so kiss, hug, and play with them, and that the bloodiest enemy can scarce have the heart to hurt them; but their ingredients of innocence and Folly, of which nature out of providence did purposely compound and blend their tender infancy, that by a frank return of pleasure they might make some sort of amends for their parents' trouble, and give in caution as it were for the discharge of a future education. The next advance from childhood is youth, and how favourably is this dealt with: how kind, courteous, and respectful are all to it? and how ready to become serviceable upon all occasions? And whence reaps it this happiness? Whence indeed, but from me only, by whose procurement it is furnished with little of wisdom, and so with the less of disquiet? And when once lads begin to grow up, and attempt to write man, their prettiness does then soon decay, their briskness flags, their humours stagnate, their jollity ceases, and their blood grows cold; and the farther they proceed in years, the more they grow backward in the enjoyment of themselves, till wasp-ish old age comes on, a burden to itself as well as others, and that so heavy and oppressive, as none would bear the weight of, unless out of pity to their sufferings I again intervene, and lend a helping hand, assisting them at a dead lift, in the same method the poets feign their gods to succour dying men, by transforming them into new creatures, which I do by bringing them back, after they have one foot in the grave, to their infancy again; so as there is a great deal of truth couched in that old pro-verb, *Bis pueri senes*— 'Once an old man, and twice a child.'   Now if any one be curious to understand what course I take to effect this alteration, my method is this: I bring them to my well of forgetfulness (the fountain whereof is in the Fortunate Islands, and the river Lethe in hell but a small stream of it), and when they have there filled their bellies full, and washed down care, by the virtue and operation thereof they become young again.   Ay, but (say you) they mere-ly dote, and play the fool: why yes, this is what I mean by growing young again: for what else is it to be a child than to be a fool and an idiot?   It is the being such that makes that age so acceptable: for who does not esteem it somewhat ominous to see a boy endowed with the discretion of a man?   And therefore for the curbing of too forward parts we have a disparaging proverb, *Odi puerulum praecoci sapientia.** And farther, who would keep company or have any thing to do with such an old blade, as, after the wear and harrowing of so many years should yet continue of as clear a head and sound a judgment as he had at any time been in his middle-age? Therefore it is great kindness of me that old men grow fools, since it is hereby only that they are freed from such vexations as would torment them if they were more wise: they can drink briskly, bear up stoutly, and lightly pass over such infirmities, as a far stronger constitution could scarce master. Sometime, with the old fellow in Plautus, they are brought back to their horn-book again, to learn to spell their fortune in love. Most wretched would they needs be if they had but wit enough to be sensible of their hard condition; but by my assistance, they carry off all well, and to their respective friends approve themselves good, sociable, jolly companions. Thus Homer makes aged Nestor famed for a smooth oily-tongued orator, while the delivery of Achilles was but rough, harsh, and hesitant; and the same poet elsewhere tells us of old men that sate on the walls, and spake with a great deal of flourish and elegance. And in this point indeed they surpass and outgo children, who are pretty forward in a soft, innocent prattle, but otherwise are too much tongue-tied, and want the others' most acceptable embellishment of a perpetual talkativeness. Add to this, that old men

*"Hateful is the youth too early wise."

love to be playing with children, and children delight as much in them, to verify the proverb, that
*Birds of a feather flock together.** And indeed
what difference can be discerned between them, but
that the one is more furrowed with wrinkles, and
has seen a little more of the world than the other?
For otherwise their whitish hair, their want of teeth,
their smallness of stature, their milk diet, their bald
crowns, their prattling, their playing, their short
memory, their heedlessness, and all their other endowments, exactly agree; and the more they advance in years, the nearer they come back to their
cradle; till, like children indeed, at last they depart
the world, without any remorse at the loss of life,
or sense of the pangs of death.

And now let any one compare the excellency of
my metamorphosing power to that which Ovid attributes to the gods. Their strange feats in some
drunken passions we will omit for their credit sake,
and instance only in such persons as they pretend
great kindness for; these they transformed into
trees, birds, insects, and sometimes serpents; but
alas, their very change into somewhat else argues the
destruction of what they were before; whereas I can
restore the same numerical man to his pristine state
of youth, health and strength. Yea, what is more,
if men would but so far consult their own interest,
as to discard all thoughts of wisdom, and entirely
resign themselves to my guidance and conduct, old
age should be a paradox, and each man's years a

Semper similem ducit deus ad similem.

perpetual spring. For look how your hard plodding students, by a close sedentary confinement to their books, grow mopish, pale, and meagre, as if, by a continual rack of brains, and torture of invention, their veins were pumped dry and their whole body squeezed sapless; whereas my followers are smooth, plump, and bucksome, and altogether as lusty as so many bacon-hogs, or sucking calves; never in their career of pleasure to be arrested with old age, if they could but keep themselves untainted from the contagiousness of wisdom, with the leprosy whereof, if at any time they are infected, it is only for prevention, lest they should otherwise have been too happy.

For a more ample confirmation of the truth of what foregoes, it is on all sides confessed, that Folly is the best preservative of youth, and the most effectual antidote against age. And it is a never-failing observation made of the people of Brabant, that, contrary to the proverb of *Older and wiser*, the more ancient they grow, the more fools they are;* and there is not any one country whose inhabitants enjoy themselves better, and rub through the world with more ease and quiet. To these are nearly related, as well by affinity of customs as of neighbourhood, my friends the Hollanders: mine I may well call them, for they stick so close and lovingly to me, that they are styled fools to a proverb, and yet scorn to be ashamed of their name.

*Gerard Lipsius, the friend of Erasmus, who wrote a commentary on the 'Praise of Folly,' evidently felt his Dutch withers a trifle wrung by this. He has to protest that no nation was humaner or better than the Brabanters, but adds that it was a jocular proverb, *Brabantus quo natu grandior, hoc stultior.*

Well, let fond mortals go now in a needless quest
of some Medea, Circe, Venus, or some enchanted
fountain, for a restorative of age, whereas the accurate performance of this feat lies only within the
ability of my art and skill. It is I only who have
the receipt of making that liquor wherewith Mem-
non's daughter lengthened out the declining days
of her grandfather Tithonus: it is I that am that
Venus, who so far restored the languishing Phaon,
as to make Sappho fall deeply in love with his
beauty. Mine are those herbs, mine those charms,
that not only lure back swift time, when past and
gone, but what is more to be admired, clip its wings,
and prevent all farther flight. So then, if you will
all agree to my verdict, that nothing is more desirable than the being young, nor any thing more
loathed than contemptible old age, you must needs
acknowledge it as an unrequitable obligation from
me, for fencing off the one, and perpetuating the
other.

But why should I confine my discourse to the
narrow subject of mankind only? View the whole
heaven itself, and then tell me what one of that
divine tribe would not be mean and despicable, if
my name did not lend him some respect and authority. Why is Bacchus always painted as a young man,
but only because he is freakish, drunk, and mad; and
spending his time in toping, dancing, masking, and
revelling, seems to have nothing in the least to do
with wisdom? Nay, so far is he from the affectation
of being accounted wise, that he is content, all the

rites of devotion which are paid unto him should consist of apishness and drollery. Farther, what scoffs and jeers did not the old comedians throw upon him? *O swinish punch-gut god*, say they, *that smells rank of the sty he was sowed up in*, and so on. But prithee, who in this case, always merry, youthful, soaked in wine, and drowned in pleasure, who, I say, in such a case, would change conditions, either with the lofty menace-looking Jove, the grave, yet timorous Pan, Pallas, of the Gorgon and the dreadful spear, or indeed any one other of heaven's landlords? Why is Cupid feigned as a boy, but only because he is an under-witted whipster, that neither acts nor thinks any thing with discretion? Why is Venus adored for the mirror of beauty, but only because she and I claim kindred, she being of the same complexion with my father Plutus, and therefore called by Homer the Golden Goddess? Beside, she imitates me in being always a laughing, if either we believe the poets, or their near kinsmen the painters, the first mentioning, the other drawing her constantly in that posture. Add farther, to what deity did the Romans pay a more ceremonial respect than to Flora, that bawd of obscenity? And if any one search the poets for an historical account of the gods, he shall find them all famous for lewd pranks and debaucheries. It is needless to insist upon the miscarriages of others, when the lecherous intrigues of Jove himself are so notorious, and when the pretendedly chaste Diana so oft uncloaked her modesty to run a hunting after her beloved Endymion. But I will say no more, for I had rather they should be told of their faults by Momus, who was wont formerly to sting them with some close reflections, till nettled by his abusive raillery, they kicked him out of heaven for his sauciness of daring to reprove such as were beyond correction: and now in his banishment from heaven he finds but cold entertainment here on earth, nay, is denied all admittance into the courts of princes, where notwithstanding my handmaid Flattery finds a most encouraging welcome: but this petulant monitor being thrust out of doors, the gods can now more freely rant and revel, and take their whole swinge of pleasure. Now the beastly Priapus may recreate himself without contradiction in lust and filthiness; now the sly Mercury may, without discovery, go on in his thieveries and nimble-fingered juggles; the sooty Vulcan may now renew his wonted custom of making the other gods laugh by his hopping so limpingly, and coming off with so many dry jokes, and biting repartees. Silenus, the old doting lover, to shew his activity, may now dance a frisking jig, and the nymphs be at the same sport naked. The goatish satyrs may make up a merry ball, and Pan, the blind harper, may put up his bagpipes, and sing bawdy catches, to which the gods, especially when they are almost drunk, shall give a most profound attention. But why should I any farther rip open and expose the weakness of the gods, a weakness so childish and absurd, that no man can at the same time keep his countenance, and make a relation of it? Now therefore, like Homer's wandering muse, I will take my leave of heaven, and come down again here below, where we shall find nothing happy, nay, nothing tolerable, without my presence and assistance. And in the first place consider how providently nature has taken care that in all her works there should be some piquant smack and relish of Folly: for since the Stoics define wisdom to be conducted by reason, and folly nothing else but the being hurried by passion, lest our life should otherwise have been too dull and inactive, that creator, who out of clay first tempered and made us up, put into the composition of our humanity more than a pound of passions to an ounce of reason; and reason he confined within the narrow cells of the brain, whereas he left passions the whole body to range in. Farther, he set up two sturdy champions to stand perpetually on the guard, that reason might make no assault, surprise, nor inroad: anger, which keeps its station in the fortress of the heart; and lust, which, like the signs Virgo and Scorpio, rules the belly and secret members. Against the forces of these two warriors how unable is reason to bear up and withstand, every day's experience does abundantly witness; while let reason be never so importunate in urging and reinforcing her admonitions to virtue, yet the passions bear all before them, and by the least offer of curb or restraint grow but more imperious, till reason itself, for quietness' sake, is forced to desist from all further remonstrance.

But because it seemed expedient that man, who

was born for the transaction of business, should
have so much wisdom as should fit and capacitate
him for the discharge of his duty herein, and yet lest
such a measure as is requisite for this purpose might
prove too dangerous and fatal, I was advised with
for an antidote, who prescribed this infallible recipe
of taking a wife, a creature so harmless and silly,
and yet so useful and convenient, as might mollify
and make pliable the stiffness and morose humour of
man. Now that which made Plato doubt under what
genus to rank woman, whether among brutes or
rational creatures, was only meant to denote the
extreme stupidity and folly of that sex, a sex so
unalterably simple, that for any of them to thrust
forward, and reach at the name of wise, is but to
make themselves the more remarkable fools, such
an endeavour being but a swimming against the
stream, nay, the turning the course of nature, the
bare attempting whereof is as extravagant as the
effecting of it is impossible: for as it is a proverb
among the Greeks, *That an ape will be an ape,
though clad in purple;* so a woman will be a woman,
i.e., a fool, whatever disguise she takes up.   And
yet there is no reason women should take it amiss
to be thus charged; for if they do but rightly consider they will find it is to Folly they are beholden
for those endowments, wherein they so far surpass
and excel man; as first, for their unparalleled beauty,
by the charm whereof they tyrannize over the greatest tyrants; for what is it but too great a smatch of
wisdom that makes men so tawny and thick-skinned,

[27]

so rough and prickly-bearded, like an emblem of winter or old age, while women have such dainty smooth cheeks, such a low gentle voice, and so pure a complexion, as if nature had drawn them for a standing pattern of all symmetry and comeliness? Beside, what greater or juster aim and ambition have they than to please their husbands? In order whereunto they garnish themselves with paint, washes, curls, perfumes, and all other mysteries of ornament; yet after all they become acceptable to them only for their folly. Wives are always allowed their humour, yet it is only in exchange for titillation and pleasure, which indeed are but other names for folly; as none can deny, who consider how a man must hug, and dandle, and kittle, and play a hundred little tricks with his bed-fellow when he is disposed to make that use of her that nature designed her for. Well, then, you see whence that greatest pleasure (to which modesty scarce allows a name) springs and proceeds.

But now some blood-chilled old men, that are more for wine than wenching, will pretend, that in their opinion the greatest happiness consists in feasting and drinking. Grant it be so; yet certainly in the most luxurious entertainments it is Folly must give the sauce and relish to the daintiest cates and delicacies; so that if there be no one of the guests naturally fool enough to be played upon by the rest, they must procure some comical buffoon, that by his jokes, and flouts, and blunders shall make the whole company split themselves with laughing: for to what pur-

pose were it to be stuffed and crammed with so many
dainty bits, savoury dishes, and toothsome rarities,
if after all this epicurism of the belly, the eyes, the
ears, and the whole mind of man, were not as well
pastured and relieved with laughing, jesting, and
such like divertisements, which like second courses
serve for the promoting of digestion?   And as to
all those shooing horns of drunkenness, the keeping
every one his man, the throwing hey-jinks, the filling
of bumpers, the drinking two in a hand, the beginning of mistress' healths; and then the roaring out
of drunken catches, the calling in a fiddler, the lead-
ing out every one his lady to dance, and such like
riotous pastimes, these were not taught or dictated
by any of the wise men of Greece, but of Gotham
rather, being my invention, and by me prescribed as
the best preservative of health: each of which, the
more ridiculous it is, the more welcome it finds.
And indeed to jog sleepingly through the world, in
a dumpish melancholy posture cannot properly be
said to live, but to be wound up as it were in a
winding-sheet before we are dead, and so to be
shuffled quick into a grave, and buried alive.

But there are yet others perhaps that have no
taste for this sort of pleasure, but place their greatest
content in the enjoyment of friends, telling us that
true friendship is to be preferred before all other
acquirements; that it is a thing so useful and necessary, as the very elements could not long subsist
without a natural combination; so pleasant that it
affords as warm an influence as the sun itself; so

honest (if honesty in this case deserve any consideration) that the very philosophers have not stuck
to place this as one among the rest of their different
sentiments of the chiefest good. But what if I
make it appear that I also am the main spring and
original of this endearment? Yes, I can easily demonstrate it, and that not by crabbed syllogisms, or a
crooked and unintelligible way of arguing, but can
make it (as the proverb goes) *As plain as the nose
on your face.* Well, then, to scratch and curry one
another, to wink at a friend's faults; nay, to cry up
some failings for virtuous and commendable, is not
this the next door to the being a fool? When one
looking stedfastly in his mistress's face, admires a
mole as much as a beauty spot; when another swears
his lady's stinking breath is a most redolent per-
fume; and at another time the fond parent hugs the
squint-eyed child, and pretends it is rather a becoming glance and winning aspect than any blemish of
the eye-sight, what is all this but the very height of
Folly? Folly (I say) that both makes friends and
keeps them so. I speak of mortal men only, among
whom there are none but have some small faults;
he is most happy that has fewest. If we pass to the
gods, we shall find that they have so much of wisdom, as they have very little of friendship; nay,
nothing of that which is true and hearty. The reason why men make a greater improvement in this
virtue, is only because they are more credulous and
easy natured; for friends must be of the same
humour and inclinations too, or else the league of

amity, though made with never so many protesta-
tions, will be soon broke.   Thus grave and morose
men seldom prove fast friends; they are too captious
and censorious, and will not bear with one another's
infirmities; they are as eagle sighted as may be in
the espial of others' faults, while they wink upon
themselves, and never mind the beam in their own
eyes.   In short, man being by nature so prone to
frailties, so humoursome and cross-grained, and
guilty of so many slips and miscarriages, there could
be no firm friendship contracted, except there be such
an allowance made for each other's defaults, which
the Greeks term Εὐήθεια, and we may construe good
nature, which is but another word for Folly.   And
what?   Is not Cupid, that first father of all relation, is not he stark blind, that as he cannot himself
distinguish of colours, so he would make us as mope-
eyed in judging falsely of all love concerns, and
wheedle us into thinking that we are always in the
right?   Thus every Jack sticks to his own Jill;
every tinker esteems his own trull; and the hob-
nailed suitor prefers Joan the milk-maid before any
of my lady's daughters.   These things are true, and
are ordinarily laughed at, and yet, however ridiculous they seem, it is hence only that all societies
receive their cement and consolidation.

The same which has been said of friendship is
much more applicable to a state of marriage, which
is but the highest advance and improvement of
friendship in the closest bond of union. Good God!
What frequent divorces, or worse mischief, would

oft sadly happen, except man and wife were so dis-
creet as to pass over light occasions of quarrel with
laughing, jesting, dissembling, and such like playing
the fool? Nay, how few matches would go forward, if the hasty lover did but first know how
many little tricks of lust and wantonness (and perhaps more gross failings) his coy and seemingly
bashful mistress had oft before been guilty of? And
how fewer marriages, when consummated, would
continue happy, if the husband were not either sottishly insensible of, or did not purposely wink at
and pass over the lightness and forwardness of his
good-natured wife? This peace and quietness is
owing to my management, for there would otherwise be continual jars, and broils, and mad doings,
if want of wit only did not at the same time make
a contented cuckold and a still house; if the cuckoo
sing at the back door, the unthinking cornute takes
no notice of the unlucky omen of others' eggs being
laid in his own nest, but laughs it over, kisses his
dear spouse, and all is well. And indeed it is much
better to be thus deceived, than always to be racked
and tortured with the grating surmises of suspicion
and jealousy. In fine, there is no one society, no
one relation men stand in, that would be comfortable, or indeed tolerable, without my assistance;
there could be no right understanding betwixt prince
and people, lord and servant, tutor and pupil, friend
and friend, man and wife, buyer and seller, or any
persons however otherwise related, if they did not
cowardly endure small abuses, sneakingly cringe and

submit, or after all fawningly scratch and flatter each other.   This you will say is much, but you shall yet hear what is more; tell me then, can any one love another that first hates himself?   Is it likely any one should agree with a friend that is first fallen out with his own judgment?   Or is it probable he should be any way pleasing to another, who is a perpetual plague and trouble to himself?   This is such a paradox that none can be so mad as to maintain.   Well, but if I am excluded and barred out, every man would be so far from being able to bear with others, that he would be burthensome to himself, and consequently incapable of any ease or satisfaction. Nature, that toward some of her products plays the stepmother rather than the indulgent parent, has endowed some men with that unhappy peevishness of disposition, as to nauseate and dislike whatever is their own, and much admire what belongs to other persons, so as they cannot in any wise enjoy what their birth or fortunes have bestowed upon them: for what grace is there in the greatest beauty, if it be always clouded with frowns and sullenness?   Or what vigour in youth, if it be harassed with a pettish, dogged, waspish, ill humour?   None, sure. Nor indeed can there be any creditable acquitting of ourselves in any one station of life, but we should sink without rescue into misery and despair, if we were not buoyed up and supported by Self-love, which is but the elder sister (as it were) of Folly, and her own constant friend and assistant.   For what is or can be more silly than to be lovers and admirers of ourselves? And yet if it were not so there will be no relish to any of our words or actions. Take away this one property of a fool, and the orator shall become as dumb and silent as the pulpit he stands in; the musician shall hang up his untouched instruments on the wall; the completest actors shall be hissed off the stage; the poet shall be burlesqued with his own doggerel rhymes; the painter shall himself vanish into an imaginary landscape; and the physician shall want food more than his patients do physic. So every deformed Thersites takes himself for a handsome Nireus, every senile Nestor for a rejuvenated Phaon, every sow for a Minerva, and every rustic for a polished citizen. In short, without self-love, instead of beautiful, you shall think yourself an old beldam of fourscore; instead of youthful, you shall seem just dropping into the grave; instead of eloquent, a mere stammerer; and in lieu of gentle and complaisant, you shall appear like a downright country clown; it being so necessary that every one should think well of himself before he can expect the good opinion of others. Finally, when it is the main and essential part of happiness to desire to be no other than what we already are; this expedient is again wholly owing to self-love, which so flushes men with a good conceit of their own, that no one repents of his shape, of his wit, of his education, or of his country; so as the dirty half-drowned Hollander would not remove into the pleasant plains of Italy, the rude Thracian would not change his boggy soil for the best seat in

Athens, nor the brutish Scythian quit his thorny
deserts to become an inhabitant of the Fortunate
Islands. And oh the incomparable contrivance of
nature, who has ordered all things in so even a
method that wherever she has been less bountiful
in her gifts, there she makes it up with a larger dose
of self-love, which supplies the former defects, and
makes all even. To enlarge farther, I may well
presume to aver, that there are no considerable exploits performed, no useful arts invented, but what
I am the author and manager of: as first, what is
more lofty and heroical than war? and yet, what is
more foolish than for some petty, trivial affront, to
take such a revenge as both sides shall be sure to be
losers, and where the quarrel must be decided at the
price of so many limbs and lives? And when they
come to an engagement, what service can be done by
such pale-faced students, as by drudging at the oars
of wisdom, have spent all their strength and activity? No, the only use is of blunt sturdy fellows
that have little of wit, and so the more of resolution; except you would make a soldier of such
another Demosthenes as, following the counsel of
Archilochus, threw down his arms when he came
within sight of the enemy, and lost that credit in
the camp which he gained in the pulpit. But counsel, deliberation, and advice (say you), are very
necessary for the management of war: very true, but
not such counsel as shall be prescribed by the strict
rules of wisdom and justice; for a battle shall be
more successfully fought by serving-men, porters,

bailiffs, padders, rogues, gaol-birds, and such like
tag-rags of mankind, than by the most accomplished
philosophers; which last, how unhappy they are in
the management of such concerns, Socrates (by the
oracle adjudged to be the wisest of mortals) is a
notable example; who when he appeared in the attempt of some public performance before the people,
he faltered in the first onset, and could never recover
himself, but was hooted and hissed home again: yet
this philosopher was the less a fool, for refusing the
appellation of wise, and not accepting the oracle's
compliment; as also for advising that no philosophers should have any hand in the government of
the commonwealth; he should have likewise at the
same time, added, that they should be banished all
human society. And what made this great man
poison himself to prevent the malice of his accusers?
What made him the instrument of his own death,
but only his excessiveness of wisdom? whereby,
while he was searching into the nature of clouds,
while he was plodding and contemplating upon
ideas, while he was exercising his geometry upon the
measure of a flea, and diving into the recesses of
nature, for an account how little insects, when they
were so small, could make so great a buzz and hum;
while he was intent upon these fooleries he minded
nothing of the world, or its ordinary concerns.

Next to Socrates comes his scholar Plato, a famous
orator indeed, that could be so dashed out of countenance by an illiterate rabble, as to demur, and
hawk, and hesitate, before he could get to the end

Three wise fools

of one short sentence. Theophrastus was such another coward, who beginning to make an oration, was presently struck down with fear, as if he had seen some ghost, or hobgoblin. Isocrates was so bashful and timorous, that though he taught rhetoric, yet he could never have the confidence to speak in public. Cicero, the master of Roman eloquence, was wont to begin his speeches with a low, quivering voice, just like a schoolboy afraid of not saying his lesson perfect enough to escape whipping: and yet Fabius commends this property of Tully as an argument of a considerate orator, sensible of the difficulty of acquitting himself with credit: but what hereby does he do more than plainly confess that wisdom is but a rub and impediment to the well management of any affair? How would these heroes crouch, and shrink into nothing, at the sight of drawn swords, that are thus quashed and stunned at the delivery of bare words?

Now then let Plato's fine sentence be cried up, that 'happy are those commonwealths where either philosophers are elected kings, or kings turn philosophers.' Alas, this is so far from being true, that if we consult all historians for an account of past ages, we shall find no princes more weak, nor any people more slavish and wretched, than where the administration of affairs fell on the shoulders of some learned bookish governor. Of the truth whereof, the two Catos are exemplary instances: the first of which embroiled the city, and tired out the senate by his tedious harangues of defending

himself, and accusing others; the younger was an
unhappy occasion of the loss of the people's liberty,
while by improper methods he pretended to maintain it.   To these may be added Brutus, Cassius,
the two Gracchi, and Cicero himself, who was no
less fatal to Rome, than his parallel Demosthenes
was to Athens: as likewise Marcus Antoninus, whom
we may allow to have been a good emperor, yet the
less such for his being a philosopher; and certainly
he did not do half that kindness to his empire by
his own prudent management of affairs, as he did
mischief by leaving such a degenerate successor as
his son Commodus proved to be; but it is a common
observation, that *A wise father has many times a
foolish son,* nature so contriving it, lest the taint of
wisdom, like hereditary distempers, should otherwise descend by propagation.   Thus Tully's son
Marcus, though bred at Athens, proved but a dull,
insipid soul; and the children of Socrates had (as
one ingeniously expresses it) "more of the mother
than the father," a phrase for their being fools.
However, it were the more excusable, though wise
men are so awkward and unhandy in the ordering
of public affairs, if they were not so bad, or worse
in the management of their ordinary and domestic
concerns; but alas, here they are much to seek: for
place a formal wise man at a feast, and he shall
either by his morose silence put the whole table out
of humour, or by his frivolous questions disoblige
and tire out all that sit near him.   Call him out to
dance, and he shall move no more nimbly than a

camel: invite him to any public performance, and
by his very looks he shall damp the mirth of all
the spectators, and at last be forced, like Cato, to
leave the theatre, because he cannot unstarch his
gravity, nor put on a more pleasant countenance.
If he engage in any discourse, he either breaks off
abruptly, or tires out the patience of the whole company, if he goes on: if he have any contract, sale, or
purchase to make, or any other worldly business to
transact, he behaves himself more like a senseless
stock than a rational man; so as he can be of no
use nor advantage to himself, to his friends, or to
his country; because he knows nothing how the
world goes, and is wholly unacquainted with the
humour of the vulgar, who cannot but hate a person
so disagreeing in temper from themselves.

And indeed the whole proceedings of the world
are nothing but one continued scene of Folly, all
the actors being equally fools and madmen: and
therefore if any be so pragmatically wise as to be
singular, he must even turn a second Timon, or
man-hater, and by retiring into some unfrequented
desert, become a recluse from all mankind.

But to return to what I first proposed, what was
it in the infancy of the world that made men, naturally savage, unite into civil societies, but only flattery,
one of my chiefest virtues? For there is nothing
else meant by the fables of Amphion and Orpheus
with their harps; the first making the stones jump
into a well-built wall, the other inducing the trees
to pull their legs out of the ground, and dance the

morrice after him. What was it that quieted and
appeased the Roman people, when they brake out
into a riot for the redress of grievances? Was it
any sinewy starched oration? No, alas, it was only
a silly, ridiculous story, told by Menenius Agrippa,
how the other members of the body quarrelled with
the belly, resolving no longer to continue her drudging caterers, till by the penance they thought thus
in revenge to impose, they soon found their own
strength so far diminished, that paying the cost of
experiencing a mistake, they willingly returned to
their respective duties. Thus when the rabble of
Athens murmured at the exaction of the magistrates, Themistocles satisfied them with such another
tale of the fox and the hedgehog: the first whereof
being stuck fast in a miry bog, the flies came swarm-
ing about him, and almost sucked out all his blood,
the latter officiously offers his services to drive them
away: no, says the fox, if these which are almost
glutted be frighted off, there will come a new hungry
set that will be ten times more greedy and devour-
ing: the moral of this he meant applicable to the
people, who if they had such magistrates removed as
they complained of for extortion, yet their successors would certainly be worse.

With what highest advances of policy could Sertorius have kept the Barbarians so well in awe, as
by a white hart, which he pretended was presented
to him by Diana, and brought him intelligence of
all his enemies' designs? What was Lycurgus his
grand argument for demonstrating the force of edu-

cation, but only the bringing out two whelps of the same bitch, differently brought up, and placing before them a dish, and a live hare; the one, that had been bred to hunting, ran after the game; while the other, whose kennel had been a kitchen, presently fell a licking the platter. Thus the before-mentioned Sertorius made his soldiers sensible that wit and contrivance would do more than bare strength, by setting a couple of men to the plucking off two horses' tails; the first pulling at all in one handful, tugged in vain; while the other, though much the weaker, snatching off one by one, soon performed his appointed task.

Instances of like nature are Minos and king Numa, both which fooled the people into obedience by a mere cheat and juggle; the first by pretending he was advised by Jupiter, the latter by making the vulgar believe he had the goddess Ægeria assistant to him in all debates and transactions. And indeed it is by such wheedles that the common people are best gulled and imposed upon.

For farther, what city would ever submit to the rigorous laws of Plato, to the severe injunctions of Aristotle? or the more unpracticable tenets of Socrates? No, these would have been too straight and galling, there not being allowance enough made for the infirmities of the people.

To pass to another head, what was it made the Decii so forward to offer themselves up as a sacrifice for an atonement to the angry gods, to rescue and stipulate for their indebted country? What made

Curtius, on a like occasion, so desperately to throw
away his life, but only vainglory, that is condemned, and unanimously voted for a main branch
of Folly by all wise men?   What is more unreasonable and foppish (say they) than for any man, out
of ambition to some office, to bow, to scrape and
cringe to the gaping rabble, to purchase their favour
by bribes and donatives, to have their names cried
up in the streets, to be carried about as it were for
a fine sight upon the shoulders of the crowd, to have
their effigies carved in brass, and put up in the mar-
ket place for a monument of their popularity?   Add
to this, the affectation of new titles and distinctive
badges of honour; nay, the very deifying of such
as were the most bloody tyrants.   These are so extremely ridiculous, that there is need of more than
one Democritus to laugh at them.   And yet hence
only have been occasioned those memorable achieve-
ments of heroes, that have so much employed the
pens of many laborious writers.

     It is Folly that, in a several dress, governs cities,
appoints magistrates, and supports judicatures; and,
in short, makes the whole course of man's life a mere
children's play, and worse than push-pin diversion.
The invention of all arts and sciences is likewise
owing to the same cause: for what sedentary,
thoughtful men would have beat their brains in the
search of new and unheard-of mysteries, if not egged
on by the bubbling hopes of credit and reputation?
They think a little glittering flash of vainglory is a
sufficient reward for all their sweat, and toil, and

tedious drudgery, while they that are supposedly more foolish, reap advantage of the others' labours.

And now since I have made good my title to valour and industry, what if I challenge an equal share of wisdom? How! this (you will say) is absurd and contradictory; fire and water may as soon be mixed as Folly and Wisdom be reconciled. Well, but have a little patience and I will warrant you I will make out my claim. First then, if wisdom (as must be confessed) is no more than a readiness of doing good, and an expedite method of becoming serviceable to the world, to whom does this virtue more properly belong? To the wise man, who partly out of modesty, partly out of cowardice, can proceed resolutely in no attempt; or to the fool, that goes hand over head, leaps before he looks, and so ventures through the most hazardous undertaking without any sense or prospect of danger? In the undertaking any enterprise the wise man shall run to consult with his books, and daze himself with poring upon musty authors, while the dispatchful fool shall rush bluntly on, and have done the business, while the other is thinking of it. For the two greatest lets and impediments to the issue of any performance are modesty, which casts a mist before men's eyes; and fear, which makes them shrink back, and recede from any proposal: both these are banished and cashiered by Folly, and in their stead such a habit of fool-hardiness introduced, as mightily contributes to the success of all enterprises. Farther, if you will have wisdom taken in the other sense, of being a right judgment of things, you shall see how short wise men fall of it in this acceptation.

First, then, it is certain that all things, like so many Januses, carry a double face, or rather bear a false aspect, most things being really in themselves far different from what they are in appearance to others: so as that which at first blush proves alive, is in truth dead; and that again which appears as dead, at a nearer view proves to be alive: beautiful seems ugly, wealthy poor, scandalous is thought creditable, prosperous passes for unlucky, friendly for what is most opposite, and innocent for what is hurtful and pernicious. In short, if we change the tables, all things are found placed in a quite different posture from what just before they appeared to stand in.

If this seem too darkly and unintelligibly expressed, I will explain it by the familiar instance of some great king or prince, whom every one shall suppose to swim in a luxury of wealth, and to be a powerful lord and master; when, alas, on the one hand he has poverty of spirit enough to make him a mere beggar, and on the other side he is worse than a galley-slave to his own lusts and passions.

If I had a mind farther to expatiate, I could enlarge upon several instances of like nature, but this one may at present suffice.

Well, but what is the meaning (will some say) of all this? Why, observe the application. If any one in a playhouse be so impertinent and rude as to rifle the actors of their borrowed clothes, make them lay down the character assumed, and force them to return to their naked selves, would not such a one wholly discompose and spoil the entertainment? And would he not deserve to be hissed and thrown stones at till the pragmatical fool could learn better manners? For by such a disturbance the whole scene will be altered: such as acted the men will perhaps appear to be women: he that was dressed up for a young brisk lover, will be found a rough old fellow; and he that represented a king, will remain but a mean ordinary serving-man. The laying things thus open is marring all the sport, which consists only in counterfeit and disguise. Now the world is nothing else but such another comedy, where every one in the tire-room is first habited suitably to the part he is to act; and as it is successively their turn, out they come on the stage, where he that now personates a prince, shall in another part of the same play alter his dress, and become a beggar, all things being in a mask and particular disguise, or otherwise the play could never be presented. Now if there should arise any starched, formal don, that would point at the several actors, and tell how this, that seems a petty god, is in truth worse than a brute, being made captive to the tyranny of passion; that the other, who bears the character of a king, is indeed the most slavish of serving-men, in being subject to the mastership of lust and sensuality; that a third, who vaunts so much of his pedigree, is no better than a bastard for degenerating from virtue, which ought to be of

greatest consideration in heraldry. and so shall go
on in exposing all the rest; would not any one
think such a person quite frantic, and ripe for bedlam? For as nothing is more silly than preposterous
wisdom, so is there nothing more indiscreet than an
unreasonable reproof. And therefore he is to be
hooted out of all society that will not be pliable,
conformable, and willing to suit his humour with
other men's, remembering the law of clubs and meet-
ings, that he who will not do as the rest must get him
out of the company. And it is certainly one great
degree of wisdom for every one to consider that he
is but a man, and therefore he should not pitch his
soaring thoughts beyond the level of mortality, but
clip the wings of his towering ambition, and oblig-
ingly submit and condescend to the weakness of
others, it being many times a piece of complaisance
to go out of the road for company's sake. No (say
you), this is a grand piece of Folly: true, but yet all
our living is no more than such kind of fooling:
which though it may seem harsh to assert, yet it is
not so strange as true.

For the better making it out it might perhaps be
requisite to invoke the aid of the muses, to whom
the poets devoutly apply themselves upon far more
slender occasions. Come then and assist, ye Heli-
conian lasses, while I attempt to prove that there is
no method for an arrival at wisdom, and consequently no track to the goal of happiness, without
the instructions and directions of Folly.

And here, in the first place it has been already

acknowledged, that all the passions are listed under my regiment, since this is resolved to be the only distinction betwixt a wise man and a fool, that this latter is governed by passion. the other guided by reason: and therefore the Stoicks look upon passions no other than as the infection and malady of the soul that disorders the constitution of the whole man, and by putting the spirits into a feverish ferment many times occasions some mortal distemper. And yet these, however decried, are not only our tutors to instruct us towards the attainment of wisdom, but even strengthen us likewise, and spur us on to a quicker dispatch of all our undertakings. 'This, I suppose, will be stomached by the stoical Seneca, who pretends that the only emblem of wisdom is the man without passion; whereas the supposing any person to be so, is perfectly to unman him, or else to transform him into some fabulous deity that never was, nor ever will be; nay, to speak more plain, it is but the making him a mere statue, immoveable, senseless, and altogether inactive. And if this be their wise man, let them take him to themselves, and remove him into Plato's commonwealth, the new Atlantis, or some other like fairy land. For who would not hate and avoid such a person as should be deaf to all the dictates of common sense? that should have no more power of love or pity than a block or stone, that remains heedless of all dangers? that thinks he can never mistake, but can foresee all contingencies at the greatest distance, and make provision for the worst presages? that feeds upon himself and his own thoughts, that monopolises health, wealth, power, dignity, and all to himself? that loves no man, nor is beloved of any? that has the impudence to tax even divine providence of ill contrivance, and proudly grudges, nay, tramples under foot all other men's reputation; and this is he that is the Stoick's complete wise man.   But prithee what city would choose such a magistrate? what army be willing to serve under such a commander? or what woman would be content with such a do-little husband? who would invite such a guest? or what servant would be retained by such a master? The most illiterate mechanic would in all respects be a more acceptable man, who would be frolicsome with his wife, free with his friends, jovial at a feast, pliable in converse, and obliging to all company.   But I am tired out with this part of my subject, and so must pass to some other topics.

And now were any one placed on that tower, from whence Jove is fancied by the poets to survey the world, he would all around discern how many grievances and calamities our whole life is on every side encompassed with: how unclean our birth, how troublesome our tendance in the cradle, how liable our childhood is to a thousand misfortunes, how toilsome and full of drudgery our riper years, how heavy and uncomfortable our old age, and lastly, how unwelcome the unavoidableness of death. Farther, in every course of life how many racks there may be of torturing diseases, how many unhappy accidents may casually occur, how many unexpected disasters may arise, and what strange alterations may one moment produce?   Not to mention such miseries as men are mutually the cause of, as poverty, imprisonment, slander, reproach, revenge, treachery, malice, cousenage, deceit, and so many more, as to reckon them all would be as puzzling arithmetic as the numbering of the sands.

How mankind became environed with such hard circumstances, or what deity imposed these plagues, as a penance on rebellious mortals, I am not now at leisure to enquire: but whoever seriously takes them into consideration must needs commend the valour of the Milesian virgins, who voluntarily killed themselves to get rid of a troublesome world: and how many wise men have taken the same course of becoming their own executioners; among whom, not to mention Diogenes, Xenocrates, Cato, Cassius, Brutus, and other heroes, the self-denying Chiron is never enough to be commended; who, when he was offered by Apollo the privilege of being exempted from death, and living on to the world's end, he refused the enticing proposal, as deservedly thinking it a punishment rather than a reward.

But if all were thus wise you see how soon the world would be unpeopled, and what need there would be of a second Prometheus, to plaister up the decayed image of mankind. √ I therefore come and stand in this gap of danger and prevent farther mischief; partly by ignorance, partly by inadvertence; by the oblivion of whatever would be grating to remember, and the hopes of whatever may be grateful to expect, together palliating all griefs with an intermixture of pleasure; whereby I make men so far from being weary of their lives, that when their thread is spun to its full length, they are yet unwilling to die, and mighty hardly brought to take their last farewell of their friends. Thus some decrepit old fellows, that look as hollow as the grave into which they are falling, that rattle in the throat at every word they speak, that can eat no meat but what is tender enough to suck, that have more hair on their beard than they have on their head, and go stooping toward the dust they must shortly return to; whose skin seems already drest into parchment, and their bones already dried to a skeleton; these shadows of men shall be wonderful ambitious of living longer, and therefore fence off the attacks of death with all imaginable sleights and impostures; one shall new dye his grey hairs, for fear their colour should betray his age; another shall spruce himself up in a light periwig; a third shall repair the loss of his teeth with an ivory set; and a fourth perhaps shall fall deeply in love with a young girl, and accordingly court her with as much of gaiety and briskness as the liveliest spark in the whole town: and we cannot but know, that for an old man to marry a young wife without a portion, to be a cooler to other men's lust, is grown so common, that it is become the à-la-mode of the times. And what is yet more comical, you shall have some wrinkled old women, whose very looks are a sufficient antidote to lechery, that shall be canting out,

Ah, life is a sweet thing, and so run a caterwauling, and hire some strong-backed stallions to recover their almost lost sense of feeling; and to set themselves off the better, they shall paint and daub their faces, always stand a tricking up themselves at their looking-glass, go naked-necked, bare-breasted, be tickled at a smutty jest, dance among the young girls, write love-letters, and do all the other little knacks of decoying hot-blooded suitors; and in the meanwhile, however they are laughed at, they enjoy themselves to the full, live up to their hearts' desire, and want for nothing that may complete their happiness. As for those that think them herein so ridiculous, I would have them give an ingenuous answer to this one query, whether if folly or hanging were left to their choice, they had not much rather live like fools, than die like dogs? But what matter is it if these things are resented by the vulgar? Their ill word is no injury to fools, who are either altogether insensible of any affront, or at least lay it not much to heart. If they were knocked on the head, or had their brains dashed out, they would have some cause to complain; but alas, slander, calumny, and disgrace are no other way injurious than as they are interpreted; nor otherwise evil, than as they are thought to be so: what harm is it then if all persons deride and scoff you, if you bear but up in your own thoughts, and be yourself thoroughly conceited of your deserts? And prithee, why should it be thought any scandal to be a fool, since the being so is one part of our nature and essence; and as so, our not being wise can no more reasonably be imputed as a fault, than it would be proper to laugh at a man because he cannot fly in the air like birds and fowls; because he goes not on all four as beasts of the field; because he does not wear a pair of visible horns as a crest on his forehead, like bulls or stags: by the same figure we may call a horse unhappy, because he was never taught his grammar; and an ox miserable, for that he never learnt to fence: but sure as a horse for not knowing a letter is nevertheless valuable, so a man, for being a fool, is never the more unfortunate, it being by nature and providence so ordained for each.

Ay, but (say our patrons of wisdom) the knowledge of arts and sciences is purposely attainable by men, that the defect of natural parts may be supplied by the help of acquired: as if it were probable that nature, which had been so exact and curious in the mechanism of flowers, herbs, and flies, should have bungled most in her masterpiece, and made man as it were by halves, to be afterward polished and refined by his own industry, in the attainment of such sciences as the Egyptians feigned were invented by their god Theuth, as a sure plague and punishment to mankind, being so far from augmenting their happiness, that they do not answer that end they were first designed for, which was the improvement of memory, as Plato in his Phædrus does wittily observe.

In the first golden age of the world there was no need of these perplexities; there was then no other sort of learning but what was naturally collected from every man's common sense, improved by an easy experience. What use could there have been of grammar, when all men spoke the same mother-tongue, and aimed at no higher pitch of oratory, than barely to be understood by each other? What need of logic, when they were too wise to enter into any dispute? Or what occasion for rhetoric, where no difference arose to require any laborious decision? And as little reason had they to be tied up by any laws, since the dictates of nature and common morality were restraint and obligation sufficient: and as to all the mysteries of providence, they made them rather the object of their wonder, than their curiosity; and therefore were not so presumptuous as to dive into the depths of nature, to labour for the solving all phenomena in astronomy, or to rack their brains in the splitting of entities, and unfolding the nicest speculations, judging it a crime for any man to aim at what is put beyond the reach of his shallow apprehension.

Thus was ignorance, in the infancy of the world, as much the parent of happiness as it has been since of devotion: but as soon as the golden age began by degrees to degenerate into more drossy metals, then were arts likewise invented; yet at first but few in number, and those rarely understood, till in farther process of time the superstition of the Chaldeans, and the curiosity of the Grecians, spawned so many subtleties, that now it is scarce the work of an age to be thoroughly acquainted with all the criticisms in grammar only. And among all the several Arts, those are proportionably most esteemed that come nearest to weakness and folly. For thus divines may bite their nails, and naturalists may blow their fingers, astrologers may know their own fortune is to be poor, and the logician may shut his fist and grasp the wind.

While all these hard-named fellows cannot make
So great a figure as a single quack.

And in this profession, those that have most confidence, though the least skill, shall be sure of the greatest custom; and indeed this whole art as it is now practised, is but one incorporated compound of craft and imposture.

Next to the physician comes (he, who perhaps will commence a suit with me for not being placed before him, I mean) the lawyer, who is so silly as to be *ignoramus* to a proverb, and yet by such are all difficulties resolved, all controversies determined, and all affairs managed so much to their own advantage, that they get those estates to themselves which they are employed to recover for their clients: while the poor divine in the mean time shall have the lice crawl upon his thread-bare gown, before, by all his sweat and drudgery, he can get money enough to purchase a new one. As those arts therefore are most advantageous to their respective professors which are farthest distant from wisdom, so are those persons incomparably most happy that have least to do with any at all, but jog on in the common road of nature, which will never mislead us, except we voluntarily leap over those boundaries which she has cautiously set to our finite beings. Nature glitters most in her own plain, homely garb, and then gives the greatest lustre when she is unsullied from all artificial garnish.

Thus if we enquire into the state of all dumb creatures, we shall find those fare best that are left to nature's conduct: as to instance in bees, what is more to be admired than the industry and contrivance of these little animals? What architect could ever form so curious a structure as they give a model of in their inimitable combs? What kingdom can be governed with better discipline than they exactly observe in their respective hives? While the horse, by turning a rebel to nature, and becoming a slave to man, undergoes the worst of tyranny: he is sometimes spurred on to battle so long till he draw his guts after him for trapping, and at last falls down, and bites the ground instead of grass; not to mention the penalty of his jaws being curbed, his tail docked, his back wrung, his sides spur-galled, his close imprisonment in a stable, his rapshin and fetters when he runs at grass, and a great many other plagues, which he might have avoided, if he had kept to that first station of freedom which nature placed him in. How much more desirable is the unconfined range of flies and birds, who living by instinct, would want nothing to complete their happiness, if some well-employed Domitian would not persecute the former, nor the sly fowler lay snares and gins for the entrapping of the other? And if young birds,

before their unfledged wings can carry them from
their nests, are caught, and pent up in a cage, for the
being taught to sing, or whistle, all their new tunes
make not half so sweet music as their wild notes, and
natural melody: so much does that which is but
rough-drawn by nature surpass and excel all the
additional paint and varnish of art. And we cannot sure but commend and admire that Pythagorean
cock, which (as Lucian relates) had been successively
a man, a woman, a prince, a subject, a fish, a horse,
and a frog; after all his experience, he summed up
his judgment in this censure, that man was the most
wretched and deplorable of all creatures, all other
patiently grazing within the enclosures of nature,
while man only broke out, and strayed beyond those
safer limits, which he was justly confined to. And
Gryllus is to be adjudged wiser than the much-coun-
selling Ulysses, in as much as when by the enchant-
ment of Circe he had been turned into a hog, he
would not lay down his swinishness, nor forsake
his beloved sty, to run the peril of a hazardous voy-
age. For a farther confirmation whereof I have the
authority of Homer, that captain of all poetry, who,
as he gives to mankind in general, the epithet of
wretched and unhappy, so he bestows in particular
upon Ulysses the title of miserable, which he never
attributes to Paris, Ajax, Achilles, or any other of
the commanders; and that for this reason, because
Ulysses was more crafty, cautious, and wise, than
any of the rest.

As those therefore fall shortest of happiness that

"Can there be any one sort of men that enjoy themselves better than those which we call idiots, changelings, fools and naturals?"

reach highest at wisdom, meeting with the greater repulse for soaring beyond the boundaries of their nature, and without remembering themselves to be but men, like the fallen angels, daring them to vie with Omnipotence, and giant-like scale heaven with the engines of their own brain; so are those most exalted in the road of bliss that degenerate nearest into brutes, and quietly divest themselves of all use and exercise of reason.

And this we can prove by a familiar instance. As namely, can there be any one sort of men that enjoy themselves better than those which we call idiots, changelings, fools and naturals? It may perhaps sound harsh, but upon due consideration it will be found abundantly true, that these persons in all circumstances fare best, and live most comfortably; as first, they are void of all fear, which is a very great privilege to be exempted from; they are troubled with no remorse, nor pricks of conscience; they are not frighted with any bugbear stories of another world; they startle not at the fancied appearance of ghosts, or apparitions; they are not racked with the dread of impending mischiefs, nor bandied with the hopes of any expected enjoyments: in short, they are unassaulted by all those legions of cares that war against the quiet of rational souls; they are ashamed of nothing, fear no man, banish the uneasiness of ambition, envy, and love; and to add the reversion of a future happiness to the enjoyment of a present one, they have no sin neither to answer for; divines unanimously maintaining, that a gross and unavoid-

able ignorance does not only extenuate and abate
from the aggravation, but wholly expiate the guilt
of any immorality.

Come now then as many of you as challenge the
respect of being accounted wise, ingenuously confess
how many insurrections of rebellious thoughts, and
pangs of a labouring mind, ye are perpetually
thrown and tortured with; reckon up all those inconveniences that you are unavoidably subject to,
and then tell me whether fools, by being exempted
from all these embroilments, are not infinitely more
free and happy than yourselves? Add to this, that
fools do not barely laugh, and sing, and play the
good-fellow alone to themselves: but as it is the
nature of good to be communicative, so they impart
their mirth to others, by making sport for the whole
company they are at any time engaged in. as if providence purposely designed them for an antidote to
melancholy: whereby they make all persons so fond
of their society, that they are welcomed to all places,
hugged, caressed, and defended, a liberty given them
of saying or doing anything: so well beloved, that
none dares to offer them the least injury; nay, the
most ravenous beasts of prey will pass them by
untouched, as if by instinct they were warned that
such innocence ought to receive no hurt. Farther,
their converse is so acceptable in the court of princes,
that few kings will banquet, walk, or take any other
diversion, without their attendance: nay. and had
much rather have their company, than that of their
gravest counsellors, whom they maintain more for

fashion-sake than good-will; nor is it so strange that these fools should be preferred before graver politicians, since these last, by their harsh, sour advice, and ill-timing the truth, are fit only to put a prince out of humour, while the others laugh, and talk, and joke, without any danger of disobliging.

It is one farther very commendable property of fools, that they always speak the truth, than which there is nothing more noble and heroical. For so, though Plato relate it as a sentence of Alcibiades, that in the sea of drunkenness truth swims uppermost, and so wine is the only teller of truth, yet this character may more justly be assumed by me, as I can make good from the authority of Euripides, who lays down this as an axiom, μωρὰ μωρὸς λέγει. Children and fools always speak the truth. Whatever the fool has in his heart he betrays it in his face; or what is more notifying, discovers it by his words: while the wise man, as Euripides observes, carries a double tongue; the one to speak what may be said, the other what ought to be; the one what truth, the other what the time requires: whereby he can in a trice so alter his judgment, as to prove that to be now white, which he had just before swore to be black; like the satyr at his porridge, blowing hot and cold at the same breath; in his lips professing one thing, when in his heart he means another.

Furthermore, princes in their greatest splendour seem upon this account unhappy, in that they miss the advantage of being told the truth, and are shammed off by a parcel of insinuating courtiers, that acquit themselves as flatterers more than as friends. But some will perchance object, that princes do not love to hear the truth, and therefore wise men must be very cautious how they behave themselves before them, lest they should take too great a liberty in speaking what is true, rather than what is acceptable. This must be confessed, truth indeed is seldom palatable to the ears of kings: yet fools have so great a privilege as to have free leave, not only to speak bare truths, but the most bitter ones too; so as the same reproof, which had it come from the mouth of a wise man would have cost him his head, being blurted out by a fool, is not only pardoned. but well taken, and rewarded. For truth has naturally a mixture of pleasure, if it carry with it nothing of offence to the person whom it is applied to; and the happy knack of ordering it so is bestowed only on fools. 'Tis for the same reason that this sort of men are more fondly beloved by women, who like their tumbling them about, and playing with them, though never so boisterously; pretending to take that only in jest, which they would have to be meant in earnest, as that sex is very ingenious in palliating, and dissembling the bent of their wanton inclinations.

But to return. An additional happiness of these fools appears farther in this, that when they have run merrily on to their last stage of life, they neither find any fear nor feel any pain to die, but march contentedly to the other world, where their com-

"Nothing more miserable than the being a fool? Alas, this is but a fallacy"

pany sure must be as acceptable as it was here upon earth.

Let us draw now a comparison between the condition of a fool and that of a wise man, and see how infinitely the one outweighs the other.

Give me any instance then of a man as wise as you can fancy him possible to be, that has spent all his younger years in poring upon books, and trudging after learning, in the pursuit whereof he squanders away the pleasantest time of his life in watching, sweating, and fasting; and in his latter days he never tastes one mouthful of delight, but is always stingy, poor, dejected, melancholy, burthensome to himself, and unwelcome to others, pale, lean, thin-jawed, sickly, contracting by his sedentariness such hurtful distempers as bring him to an untimely death, like roses plucked before they shatter. Thus have you the draught of a wise man's happiness, more the object of a commiserating pity, than of an ambitioning envy.

But now again come the croaking Stoicks, and tell me in mood and figure, that nothing is more miserable than the being mad: but the being a fool is the being mad, therefore there is nothing more miserable than the being a fool. Alas, this is but a fallacy, the discovery whereof solves the force of the whole syllogism. Well then, they argue subtlely, 'tis true; but as Socrates in Plato makes two Venuses and two Cupids, and shews how their actions and properties ought not to be confounded; so these disputants, if they had not been mad themselves, should have

distinguished between a double madness in others:
and there is certainly a great difference in the nature
as well as in the degrees of them, and they are not
both equally scandalous: for Horace seems to take
delight in one sort when he says:—

Does welcome frenzy make me thus mistake?

And Plato in his Phædo ranks the madness of
poets, of prophets, and of lovers among those properties which conduce to a happy life. And Virgil,
in the sixth Æneid, gives this epithet to his industrious Æneas:—

If you will proceed to these your mad attempts.

And indeed there is a twofold sort of madness:
the one that which the furies bring from hell; those
that are herewith possessed are hurried on to wars
and contentions, by an inexhaustible thirst of power
and riches, inflamed to some infamous and unlawful
lust, enraged to act the parricide, seduced to become
guilty of incest, sacrilege, or some other of those
crimson-dyed crimes; or, finally, to be so pricked in
conscience as to be lashed and stung with the whips
and snakes of grief and remorse. But there is another sort of madness that proceeds from Folly, so
far from being any way injurious or distasteful that
it is thoroughly good and desirable; and this happens when by a harmless mistake in the judgment
of things the mind is freed from those cares which
would otherwise gratingly afflict it, and smoothed
over with a content and satisfaction it could not
under other circumstances so happily enjoy. And
this is that comfortable apathy or insensibleness

which Cicero, in an epistle to his friend Atticus, wishes himself master of, that he might the less take to heart those insufferable outrages committed by the tyrannizing triumvirate. Lepidus, Antonius, and Augustus. That Grecian likewise had a happy time of it, who was so frantic as to sit a whole day in the empty theatre laughing, shouting, and clapping his hands, as if he had really seen some pathetic tragedy acted to the life, when indeed all was no more than the strength of imagination, and the efforts of delusion, while in all other respects the same person behaved himself very discreetly, and was

Sweet to his friends, to his wife, obliging, kind,
And so averse from a revengeful mind,
That had his men unsealed his bottled wine,
He would not fret, nor doggedly repine.

And when by a course of physic he was recovered from his frenzy, he looked upon his cure so far from a kindness, that he thus reasons the case with his friends:

This remedy, my friends, is worse i' th' main
Than the disease, the cure augments the pain;
My only hope is a relapse again.

And certainly they were the more mad of the two who endeavoured to bereave him of so pleasing a delirium, and recall all the aches of his head by dispelling the mists of his brain.

I have not yet determined whether it be proper to include all the defects of sense and understanding under the common name of madness. For if any one be so short-sighted as to take a mule for an ass,

or so shallow-pated as to admire a paltry ballad
for an elegant poem, he is not thereupon immediately censured as mad. But if any one let not only
his senses but his judgment be imposed upon in the
most ordinary common concerns, he shall come
under the scandal of being thought next door
to a madman. As suppose any one should hear an
ass bray, and should take it for ravishing music; or
if any one, born a beggar, should fancy himself to
be Crœsus, king of Lydia, or the like. But this
sort of madness, if (as is most usual) it be accompanied with pleasure, brings a great satisfaction both
to those who are possessed with it themselves, and
those who deride it in others, though they are not
both equally frantic. And this species of madness
is of larger extent than the world commonly
imagines. Thus the whole tribe of madmen make
sport among themselves, while one laughs at another; he that is more mad many times jeering him
that is less so. But indeed the greater each man's
madness is, the greater is his happiness, if it be but
such a sort as proceeds from an excess of folly, which
is so epidemical a distemper that it is hard to find any
one man so uninfected as not to have sometimes a
fit or two of some sort of frenzy. There is only
this difference between the several patients: he that
shall take a broom-stick for a strait-bodied woman
is without more ado sentenced for a madman, because this is so strange a blunder as very seldom happens; whereas he whose wife is a common jilt, that
keeps a warehouse free for all customers, and yet

swears she is as chaste as Penelope, and hugs himself
in his contented mistake, is scarce taken notice of,
because he fares no worse than a great many more of
his good-natured neighbours. Among these are to
be ranked such as take an immoderate delight in
hunting, and think no music comparable to the
sounding of horns and the yelping of beagles; even
the odour of the excrement of dogs is as cinnamon to
them. When they have run down their game, what
strange pleasure they take in cutting of it up! Cows
and sheep may be slaughtered by common butchers,
but what is killed in hunting must be broke up by
none under a gentleman, who shall throw down
his hat, fall devoutly on his knees, and drawing out
a slashing hanger (for a common knife is not good
enough), after several ceremonies shall dissect all
the parts in a prescribed order, while all that stand
round shall look very intently, and seem to be
mightily surprised with the novelty, though they
have seen the same an hundred times before; and he
that can but dip his finger, and taste of the blood,
shall think his own bettered by it: and though the
constant feeding on such diet does but assimilate
them to the nature of those beasts they eat of, yet
they will swear that venison is meat for princes, and
that their living upon it makes them as great as
emperors.

Near akin to these are such as take a great fancy
for building: they raise up, pull down, begin anew,
alter the model, and never rest till they run themselves out of their whole estate, taking up such a

compass for buildings, till they leave themselves not one foot of land to live upon, nor one poor cottage to shelter themselves from cold and hunger: and yet all the while are mighty proud of their contrivances, and sing a sweet *requiem* to their own happiness.

To these are to be added those plodding virtuosos, that plunder the most inward recesses of nature for the pillage of a new invention, and rake over sea and land for the turning up some hitherto latent mystery; and are so continually tickled with the hopes of success, that they spare for no cost nor pains, but trudge on, and upon a defeat in one attempt, courageously tack about to another, and fall upon new experiments, never giving over till they have calcined their whole estate to ashes, and have not money enough left unmelted to purchase one crucible or limbeck. And yet after all, they are not so much discouraged, but that they dream fine things still, and animate others what they can to the like undertakings; nay, when their hopes come to the last gasp, after all their disappointments, they have yet one *salvo* for their credit, that

In great exploits our bare attempts suffice.

And so inveigh against the shortness of their life, which allows them not time enough to bring their designs to maturity and perfection.

Whether dice-players may be so favourably dealt with as to be admitted among the rest is scarce yet resolved upon: but sure it is hugely vain and ridiculous, when we see some persons so devoutly addicted to this diversion, that at the first rattle of the box

their heart shakes within them, and keeps consort
with the motion of the dice: they are egg'd on so
long with the hopes of always winning, till at last,
in a literal sense, they have thrown away their whole
estate, and made shipwreck of all they have, scarce
escaping to shore with their own clothes to their
backs; thinking it in the meanwhile a great piece of
religion to be just in the payment of their stakes, and
will cheat any creditor sooner than him who trusts
them in play.   And that poring old men, that cannot tell their cast without the help of spectacles,
should be sweating at the same sport; nay, that such
decrepit blades, as by the gout have lost the use of
their fingers, should look over, and hire others to
throw for them: this indeed is prodigiously extravagant; but the consequence of it ends so oft in downright madness, that it seems rather to belong to the
Furies than to Folly.

The next to be placed among the regiment of
fools are such as make a trade of telling or inquiring
after incredible stories of miracles and prodigies:
never fearing that a lie will choke them, they will
muster up a thousand several strange relations of
spirits, ghosts, apparitions, raising of the devil, and
such like bugbears of superstition, which the farther
they are from being probably true, the more greedily
they are swallowed, and the more devoutly believed.
And these absurdities do not only bring an empty
pleasure, and cheap diversion, but they are a good
trade, and procure a comfortable income to such
priests and friars as by this craft get their gain.   To

these again are nearly related such others as attribute strange virtues to the shrines and images of saints and martyrs, and so would make their credulous proselytes believe, that if they pay their devotion to St. Christopher in the morning, they shall be guarded and secured the day following from all dangers and misfortunes: if soldiers, when they first take arms, shall come and mumble over a set prayer before the picture of St. Barbara, they shall return safe from all engagements: or if any pray to Erasmus on such particular holidays, with the ceremony of wax candles, and other fopperies, he shall in a short time be rewarded with a plentiful increase of wealth and riches. The Christians have now their gigantic St. George, as well as the pagans had their Hercules; they paint the saint on horseback, and drawing the horse in splendid trappings, very gloriously accoutred, they scarce refrain in a literal sense from worshipping the very beast.

What shall I say of such as cry up and maintain the cheat of pardons and indulgences? that by these compute the time of each soul's residence in purgatory, and assign them a longer or shorter continuance, according as they purchase more or fewer of these paltry pardons, and saleable exemptions? Or what can be said bad enough of others, who pretend that by the force of such magical charms, or by the fumbling over their beads in the rehearsal of such and such petitions (which some religious impostors invented, either for diversion, or what is more likely for advantage), they shall procure riches, honour,

The sale of indulgences

pleasure, health, long life, a lusty old age, nay, after death a sitting at the right hand of our Saviour in His kingdom; though as to this last part of their happiness, they care not how long it be deferred, having scarce any appetite toward a tasting the joys of heaven, till they are surfeited, glutted with, and can no longer relish their enjoyments on earth. By this easy way of purchasing pardons, any notorious highwayman, any plundering soldier, or any bribe-taking judge, shall disburse some part of their un-just gains, and so think all their grossest impieties sufficiently atoned for; so many perjuries, lusts, drunkennesses, quarrels, bloodsheds, cheats, treacher-ies, and all sorts of debaucheries, shall all be, as it were, struck a bargain for, and such a contract made, as if they had paid off all arrears, and might now begin upon a new score.

And what can be more ridiculous, than for some others to be confident of going to heaven by repeat-ing daily those seven verses out of the Psalms, which the devil taught St. Bernard, thinking thereby to have put a trick upon him, but that he was over-reached in his cunning.

Several of these fooleries, which are so gross and absurd, as I myself am even ashamed to own, are practised and admired, not only by the vulgar, but by such proficients in religion as one might well ex-pect should have more wit.

From the same principles of folly proceeds the custom of each country's challenging their particular guardian-saint; nay, each saint has his distinct office

allotted to him, and is accordingly addressed to upon
the respective occasions: as one for the tooth-ache, a
second to grant an easy delivery in child-birth, a
third to help persons to recover stolen goods, another
to protect seamen from shipwreck, a fifth to guard
the farmer's cows and sheep, and so on; for to rehearse all instances would be extremely tedious.

There are some more catholic saints petitioned to
upon all occasions, as more especially the Virgin
Mary, whose blind devotees think it manners now
to place the mother before the Son.*

And of all the prayers and intercessions that are
made to these respective saints the substance of them
is no more than downright Folly. Among all the
trophies that for tokens of gratitude are hung upon
the walls and ceilings of churches, you shall find no
relics presented as a memorandum of any that were
ever cured of Folly, or had been made one dram the
wiser. One perhaps after shipwreck got safe to
shore; another recovered when he had been run
through by an enemy; one, when all his fellow soldiers were killed upon the spot, as cunningly perhaps
as cowardly, made his escape from the field; another,

*In the commentary of Lipsius (which was partly inspired by Eras-
mus himself), by way of toning down this rather daring criticism, it is
explained that many ignorant people thought they could obtain by prayer
to the Virgin what it would be idle to petition Christ for. And it is
seriously added that a tablet had been seen on the wall of a church in
Italy, placed there as an expression of gratitude by a man who, having
been desperately ill, so that he had no hope from his doctor, *and not
much from God*, was nevertheless saved by the Virgin. ". . . Vide
in æde sacra affixum epigramma, in quo quidam testabatur se gravissima
febri correptum, nihil spei collocasse in medico, non multum in deo, sed
tamen divae virginis ope revixisse. Nulla, inquit, erat in medico spes,
neque multa in deo." And the commentator adds drily, "Nam hunc
versiculum forte memoria teneo."

*The devil teaching Psalms to
St. Bernard*

while he was hanging, the rope broke, and so he saved
his neck, and renewed his license for practising his
old trade of thieving; another broke gaol, and got
loose; a patient, against his physician's will, recovered of a dangerous fever; another drank poison,
which putting him into a violent looseness, did his
body more good than hurt, to the great grief of his
wife, who hoped upon this occasion to have become
a joyful widow; another had his waggon overturned,
and yet none of his horses lamed; another had caught
a grievous fall, and yet recovered from the bruise;
another had been tampering with his neighbour's
wife, and escaped very narrowly from being caught
by the enraged cuckold in the very act.   After all
these acknowledgments of escapes from such singular dangers, there is none (as I have before intimated) that return thanks for being freed from
Folly; Folly being so sweet and luscious, that it is
rather sued for as a happiness, than deprecated as a
punishment.   But why should I launch out into so
wide a sea of superstitions?

> Had I as many tongues as Argus eyes,
> Briareus hands, they all would not suffice
> Folly in all her shapes t'epitomize:

—almost all Christians being wretchedly enslaved
to blindness and ignorance, which the priests are so
far from preventing or removing, that they blacken
the darkness, and promote the delusion; wisely fore-
seeing that the people (like cows, which never give
down their milk so well as when they are gently
stroked), would part with less if they knew more,

their bounty proceeding only from a mistake of charity. Now if any grave wise man should stand up, and unseasonably speak the truth, telling every one that a pious life is the only way of securing a happy death; that the best title to a pardon of our sins is purchased by a hearty abhorrence of our guilt, and sincere resolutions of amendment; that the best devotion which can be paid to any saints is to imitate them in their exemplary life: if he should proceed thus to inform them of their several mistakes, there would be quite another estimate put upon tears, watchings, masses, fastings, and other severities, which before were so much prized, as persons will now be vexed to lose that satisfaction they formerly found in them.

In the same predicament of fools are to be ranked such, as while they are yet living, and in good health, take so great a care how they shall be buried when they die, that they solemnly appoint how many torches, how many escutcheons, how many gloves to be given, and how many mourners they will have at their funeral; as if they thought they themselves in their coffins could be sensible of what respect was paid to their corpse; or as if they doubted they should rest a whit the less quiet in the grave if they were with less state and pomp interred.

Now though I am in so great haste, as I would not willingly be stopped or detained, yet I cannot pass by without bestowing some remarks upon another sort of fools; who, though their first descent was perhaps no better than from a tapster or tinker,

yet highly value themselves upon their birth and
parentage.   One fetches his pedigree from Æneas,
another from Brute, a third from king Arthur: they
hang up their ancestors' worm-eaten pictures as records of antiquity, and keep a long list of their predecessors, with an account of all their offices and
titles, while they themselves are but transcripts of
their forefathers' dumb statues, and degenerate
even into those very beasts which they carry in their
coat of arms as ensigns of their nobility: and yet by
a strong presumption of their birth and quality, they
live not only the most pleasant and unconcerned
themselves, but there are not wanting others too
who cry up these brutes almost equal to the gods.

   But why should I dwell upon one or two instances of Folly, when there are so many of like
nature?   Conceitedness and self-love make many
by strength of fancy believe themselves happy,
when otherwise they are really wretched and despicable.   Thus the most ape-faced, ugliest fellow in the
whole town, shall think himself a Nireus, a mirror
of beauty: another shall be so proud of his parts,
that if he can but mark out a triangle with a pair of
compasses, he thinks he has mastered all the difficulties of geometry, and could outdo Euclid himself.
A third shall admire himself for a ravishing musician, though he have no more skill in the handling
of any instrument than a pig playing on the
organs: and another that rattles in the throat as
hoarse as a cock crows, shall be proud of his voice,
and think he sings like a nightingale.

E R A S M U S

There is another very pleasant sort of madness, whereby persons assume to themselves whatever accomplishment they discern in others. Thus the happy rich churl in Seneca, who had so short a memory, as he could not tell the least story without a servant standing by to prompt him, and was at the same time so weak that he could scarce go upright, yet he thought he might adventure to accept a challenge to a duel, because he kept at home some lusty, sturdy fellows, whose strength he relied upon instead of his own.

It is almost needless to insist upon the several professors of arts and sciences, who are all so egregiously conceited, that they would sooner give up their title to an estate in lands, than part with the reversion of their wits: among these, more especially stage-players, musicians, orators, and poets, each of which, the more of duncery they have, and the more of pride, the greater is their ambition: and how notoriously dull soever they be, they meet with their admirers; nay, the more silly they are the higher they are extolled; Folly (as we have before intimated) never failing of respect and esteem. If therefore every one, the more ignorant he is, the greater satisfaction he is to himself and the more commended by others, to what purpose is it to sweat and toil in the pursuit of true learning, which shall cost so many gripes and pangs of the brain to acquire, and when obtained, shall only make the laborious student more uneasy to himself, and less acceptable to others?

As nature in her dispensation of conceitedness has

The angelic hypocrite

dealt with private persons, so has she given a particular smatch of self-love to each country and nation.   Upon this account it is that the English challenge the prerogative of having the most handsome
women, of the being most accomplished in the skill
of music, and of keeping the best tables: the Scotch
brag of their gentility and relation to royalty, and
pretend the genius of their native soil inclines them
to be good disputants: the French think themselves
remarkable for complaisance and good breeding: the
Sorbonists of Paris pretend before any others to have
made the greatest proficiency in polemic divinity:
the Italians value themselves for learning and eloquence; and like the Grecians of old, account all the
world barbarians in respect of themselves; to which
piece of vanity the inhabitants of Rome are more
especially addicted, pretending themselves to be own-
ers of all those heroic virtues which their city so
many ages since was deservedly famous for.   The
Venetians stand upon their birth and pedigree.   The
Grecians pride themselves in having been the first
inventors of most arts, and in their country being
famed for the product of so many eminent philosophers.   The Turks, and all the other refuse of Ma-
hometism, pretend they profess the only true religion, and laugh at all Christians for superstitious,
narrow-souled fools.   The Jews to this day expect
their Messias as devoutly as they believe in their
first prophet Moses.   The Spaniards challenge the
repute of being accounted good soldiers.   And the
Germans are noted for their tall, proper stature, and

for their skill in magick. But not to mention any more, I suppose you are already convinced how great an improvement and addition to the happiness of human life is occasioned by self-love: the sister to which is flattery; for as self-love is nothing but the coaxing up of ourselves, so the same currying and humouring of others is termed flattery.

Flattery, it is true, is now looked upon as a scandalous name, but it is by such only as mind words more than things. They are prejudiced against it upon this account, because they suppose it justles out all truth and sincerity; whereas indeed its property is quite contrary, as appears from the examples of several brute creatures. What is more fawning than a spaniel? And yet what is more faithful to his master? What is more fond and loving than a tame squirrel? And yet what is more sporting and inoffensive? This little frisking creature is kept up in a cage to play withal, while lions, tigers, leopards, and such other savage emblems of rapine and cruelty are shewn only for state and rarity, and otherwise yield no pleasure to their respective keepers.

There is indeed a pernicious destructive sort of flattery wherewith rookers and sharks work their several ends upon such as they can make a prey of, by decoying them into traps and snares beyond recovery: but that which is the effect of folly is of a much different nature; it proceeds from a softness of spirit, and a flexibleness of good humour, and comes far nearer to virtue than that other extreme of

*"Pleasant to see how the asses
rub and scratch one another"*

friendship, namely, a stiff, sour, dogged moroseness:
it refreshes our minds when tired, enlivens them
when melancholy, reinforces them when languishing, invigorates them when heavy, recovers them
when sick, and pacifies them when rebellious: it puts
us in a method how to procure friends, and how to
keep them; it entices children to swallow the bitter
rudiments of learning; it gives a new ferment to the
almost stagnated souls of old men; it both reproves
and instructs princes without offence under the mask
of commendation: in short, it makes every man fond
and indulgent of himself, which is indeed no small
part of each man's happiness, and at the same time
renders him obliging and complaisant in all company, where it is pleasant to see how the asses rub
and scratch one another.

This again is a great accomplishment to an orator,
a greater to a physician, and the only one to a poet:
in fine, it is the best sweetener to all afflictions, and
gives true relish to the otherwise insipid enjoyments
of our whole life. Ay, but (say you) to flatter is to
deceive, and to deceive is very harsh and hurtful: no,
rather just contrary; nothing is more welcome and
bewitching than the being deceived. They are much
to be blamed for an undistinguishing head, that
make a judgment of things according to what they
are in themselves, when their whole nature consists
barely in the opinions that are had of them. For
all sublunary matters are enveloped in such a cloud
of obscurity, that the short-sightedness of human
understanding cannot pry through and arrive to

any comprehensive knowledge of them: hence the sect of Academic philosophers have modestly resolved, that all things being no more than probable, nothing can be known as certain; or if there could, yet would it but interrupt and abate from the pleasure of a more happy ignorance. Finally, our souls are so fashioned and moulded, that they are sooner captivated by appearances, than by real truths; of which, if any one would demand an example, he may find a very familiar one in churches, where, if what is delivered from the pulpit be a grave, solid, rational discourse, all the congregation grow weary, and fall asleep, till their patience be released; whereas if the preacher (pardon the impropriety of the word, the prater I would have said) be zealous, in his thumps of the cushion, antic gestures, and spend his glass* in the telling of pleasant stories, his beloved shall then stand up, tuck their hair behind their ears, and be very devoutly attentive. So among the saints, those are most resorted to who are most romantic and fabulous: as for instance, a poetic St. George, a St. Christopher, or a St. Barbara, shall be oftener prayed to than St. Peter, St. Paul, nay perhaps than Christ himself; but this, it is possible, may more properly be referred to another place.

In the mean while observe what a cheap purchase of happiness is made by the strength of fancy. For whereas many things even of inconsiderable value, would cost a great deal of pains and perhaps pelf, to procure; opinion spares charges, and yet gives us

*The hour-glass by which sermons were timed.

them in as ample a manner by conceit, as if we possessed them in reality. Thus he who feeds on such a stinking dish of fish, as another must hold his nose at a yard's distance from, yet if he feed heartily, and relish them palatably, they are to him as good as if they were fresh caught: whereas on the other hand, if any one be invited to never so dainty a joul of sturgeon, if it go against his stomach to eat any, he may sit a-hungry, and bite his nails with greater appetite than his victuals. If a woman be never so ugly and nauseous, yet if her husband can but think her a Venus, it is all one to him as if she really were so: if any man have never so ordinary and smutty a draught, yet if he admires the excellency of it, and can suppose it to have been drawn by some Apelles or Zeuxis, he is as proud of it as if it had really been done by one of their hands. I knew a friend of mine* that presented his bride with several false and counterfeit stones, making her believe that they were right jewels, and cost him so many hundred thousand crowns; under his deception the poor woman was as choice of pebbles, and painted glass, as if they had been so many natural rubies and diamonds, while the subtle husband saved a great deal in his pocket, and yet made his wife as well pleased as if he had been at ten hundred times the cost. What difference is there between them that in the darkest dungeon, can as in a platonic mirror† survey the whole world in idea, and him that stands in the open

*The commentator hints that the friend in question was "a party by the name of More."
†The allusion is to the allegory of the cave, in the 'Republic.'

air, and takes a less deluding prospect of the universe? If the beggar in Lucian, that dreamt he was a prince, had never waked, his imaginary kingdom had been as great as a real one. Between him therefore that truly is happy, and him that thinks himself so, there is no perceivable distinction; or if any, the fool has the better of it: first because his happiness costs him less, standing him only in the price of a single thought; and then, secondly, because he has more companions and partakers of his good fortune: for no enjoyment is comfortable where the benefit is not imparted to others; nor is any one station of life desirable, where we can have no converse with persons of the same condition with ourselves: and yet this is the hard fate of wise men, who are grown so scarce, that like Phœnixes, they appear but one in an age. The Grecians, it is true, reckoned up seven within the narrow precincts of their own country; yet I believe, were they to cast up their accounts anew, they would not find a half, nay, not a third part, of one in far larger extent.

Farther, when among the several good properties of Bacchus this is looked upon as the chief, namely, that he drowns the cares and anxieties of the mind, though it be indeed but for a short while; for after a small nap, when our brains are a little settled, they all return to their former corrodings: how much greater is the more durable advantage which I bring? while by one uninterrupted fit of being drunk in conceit, I perpetually cajole the mind with riots, revels, and all the excess and energy of joy.

*"That high and mighty goddess
who . . . gives to all that ask"*

Add to this, that I am so communicative and
bountiful, as to let no one particular person pass
without some token of my favour; whereas other
deities bestow their gifts sparingly to their elect only.
Bacchus has not thought fit that every soil should
bear the same juice-yielding grape: Venus has not
given to all a like portion of beauty: Mercury en-
dows but few with the knack of an accomplished
eloquence: Hercules gives not to all the same measure
of wealth and riches: Jupiter has ordained but a
few to be born to a kingdom: Mars in battle gives a
complete victory but to one party; nay, he often
makes them both losers: Apollo does not answer the
expectation of all that consult his oracles: Jove oft
thunders: Phœbus sometimes shoots the plague, or
some other infection, at the point of his darts: and
Neptune swallows down more than he bears up:
not to mention their Ve-Jupiters, their Plutos, their
Ate, goddess of loss, their evil geniuses, and such
other monsters of divinity, as had more of the hang-
man than the god in them, and were worshipped
only to deprecate that hurt which used to be inflicted
by them: I say, not to mention these, I am that high
and mighty goddess, whose liberality is of as large
an extent as her omnipotence: I give to all that ask:
I never appear sullen, nor out of humour, nor ever
demand any atonement or satisfaction for the omission of any ceremonious punctilio in my worship:
I do not storm or rage, if mortals, in their addresses
to the other gods pass me by unregarded, without
the acknowledgment of any respect or application:

whereas all the other gods are so scrupulous and exact, that it often proves less dangerous manfully to despise them, than sneakingly to attempt the difficulty of pleasing them. Thus some men are of that captious, froward humour, that a man had better be wholly strangers to them, than never so intimate friends.

Well, but there are none (say you) build any altars, or dedicate any temple to Folly. I admire (as I have before intimated) that the world should be so wretchedly ungrateful. But I am so good natured as to pass by and pardon this seeming affront, though indeed the charge thereof, as unnecessary, may well be saved: for to what purpose should I demand the sacrifice of frankincense, cakes, goats, and swine, since all persons everywhere pay me that more acceptable service, which all divines agree to be more effectual and meritorious, namely, an imitation of my communicable attributes? I do not therefore any way envy Diana for having her altars bedewed with human blood: I think myself then most religiously adored, when my respective devotees (as is their usual custom) conform themselves to my practice, transcribe my pattern, and so live the copy of me their original. And truly this pious devotion is not so much in use among Christians as is much to be wished it were: for how many zealous votaries are there that pay so profound respect to the Virgin Mary, as to place lighted tapers even at noon day upon her altars? And yet how few of them copy after her untouched chastity, her modesty, and

her other commendable virtues, in the imitation
whereof consists the truest esteem of divine worship?
Farther, why should I desire a temple, since the
whole world is but one ample continued choir, entirely dedicated to my use and service?   Nor do I
lack worshippers save at places where the earth lacks
inhabitants.   And as to the manner of my worship,
I am not yet so irrecoverably foolish, as to be prayed
to by proxy, and to have my honour intermediately
bestowed upon senseless images and pictures, which
quite subvert the true end of religion; while the
unwary supplicants seldom distinguish betwixt the
things themselves and the divinities they represent.
The same respect in the meanwhile is paid to me in
a more legitimate manner; for to me there are as
many statues erected as there are moving fabrics of
mortality; every person, even against his own will,
carrying the image of me, *i.e.*, the signal of Folly,
instamped on his countenance.   I have not therefore
the least tempting inducement to envy the more
seeming state and splendour of the other gods, who
are worshipped at set times and places; as Phœbus
at Rhodes, Venus in her Cyprian isle, Juno in the
city of Argos, Minerva at Athens, Jupiter on the
hill Olympus, Neptune at Tarentum, and Priapus
in the town of Lampsacum; while my worship ex-
tending as far as my influence, the whole world is
my one altar, whereon the most valuable incense
and sacrifice is perpetually offered up.

But lest I should seem to speak this with more of
confidence than truth, let us take a nearer view of

the mode of men's lives, whereby it will be rendered more apparently evident what largesses I everywhere bestow, and how much I am respected and esteemed of persons, from the highest to the basest quality. For the proof whereof, it being too tedious to insist upon each particular, I shall only mention such in general as are most worthy the remark, from which by analogy we may easily judge of the remainder. And indeed to what purpose would it be singly to recount the commonalty and rabble of mankind, who beyond all question are entirely on my side? and for a token of their vassalage do wear my livery in so many older shapes, and more newly invented modes of Folly, that the lungs of a thousand Democrituses would never hold out to such a laughter as this subject would excite; and to these thousand must be superadded one more, to laugh at them as much as they do at the other.

It is indeed almost incredible to relate what mirth, what sport, what diversion, the grovelling inhabitants here on earth give to the above-seated gods in heaven: for these exalted deities spend their fasting sober hours in listening to those petitions that are offered up, and in succouring such as they are appealed to by for redress; but when they are a little entered at a glass of nectar, they then throw off all serious concerns, and go and place themselves on the ascent of some promontory in heaven, and from thence survey the little mole-hill of earth. And trust me, there cannot be a more delightsome prospect, than to view such a theatre so stuffed and

*"Nothing so desirable as sleep
and idleness"*

crammed with swarms of fools. One falls desperately in love, and the more he is slighted the more
does his spaniel-like passion increase; another
is wedded to wealth rather than to a wife; a third
pimps for his own spouse, and is content to be a
cuckold so he may wear his horns gilt; a fourth is
haunted with a jealousy of his visiting neighbours;
another sobs and roars, and plays the child, for the
death of a friend or relation; and lest his own tears
should not rise high enough to express the torrent of
his grief, he hires other mourners to accompany the
corpse to the grave, and sing its *requiem* in sighs and
lamentations; another hypocritically weeps at the
funeral of one whose death at heart he rejoices for;
here a gluttonous cormorant, whatever he can scrape
up, thrusts all into his guts to pacify the cryings of
a hungry stomach; there a lazy wretch sits yawning
and stretching, and thinks nothing so desirable as
sleep and idleness; some are extremely industrious
in other men's business, and sottishly neglectful of
their own; some think themselves rich because their
credit is great, though they can never pay, till they
break, and compound for their debts; one is so
covetous that he lives poor to die rich; one for a
little uncertain gain will venture to cross the rough-
est seas, and expose his life for the purchase of a
livelihood; another will depend on the plunders of
war, rather than on the honest gains of peace; some
will close with and humour such warm old blades
as have a good estate, and no children of their own
to bestow it upon; others practice the same art of

wheedling upon good old women, that have hoarded and coffered up more bags than they know how to dispose of; both of these sly flatterers make fine sport for the gods, when they are beat at their own weapons, and (as oft happens) are gulled by those very persons they intended to make a prey of. There is another sort of base scoundrels in gentility, such scraping merchants, who although for the better vent of their commodities they lie, swear, cheat, and practice all the intrigues of dishonesty, yet think themselves no way inferior to persons of the highest quality, only because they have raked together a plentiful estate; and there are not wanting such insinuating hangers on, as shall caress and compliment them with the greatest respect, in hopes to go snacks in some of their dishonest gains; there are others so infected with the philosophical paradox of banishing property, and having all things in common, that they make no conscience of fastening on, and purloining whatever they can get, and converting it to their own use and possession; there are some who are rich only in wishes, and yet while they barely dream of vast mountains of wealth, they are as happy as if their imaginary fancies commenced real truths; some put on the best side outermost, and starve themselves at home to appear gay and splendid abroad; one with an open-handed freedom spends all he lays his fingers on; another by hook or crook catches at and grasps all he can come within the reach of; one apes it about in the streets to court popularity; another consults his ease, and sticks to the confine-

The "impertinent" pilgrim

ment of a chimney-corner; many others are tugging
hard at law for a trifle, and drive on an endless suit,
only to enrich a deferring judge, or a knavish advo-
cate; one is for new-modelling a settled government;
another is for some notable heroical attempt; and a
third by all means must travel a pilgrim to Rome,
Jerusalem, or some shrine of a saint elsewhere,
though he have no other business than the paying of
a formal impertinent visit, leaving his wife and
children to fast, while he himself forsooth is gone
to pray. In short, if (as Lucian fancies Menippus
to have done heretofore) any man could now again
look down from the orb of the moon, he would see
thick swarms as it were of flies and gnats, that were
quarrelling with each other, jostling, fighting, flut-
tering, skipping, playing, just new produced, soon
after decaying and then immediately vanishing; and
it can scarce be thought how many tumults and
tragedies so inconsiderable a creature as man does
give occasion to, and that in so short a space as the
small span of life; subject to so many casualties,
that the sword, pestilence, and other epidemic accidents, shall many times sweep away whole thou-
sands at a brush.

But hold; I should but expose myself too far,
and incur the guilt of being roundly laughed at, like
Democritus, if I should proceed to enumerate the
several kinds of the folly of the vulgar. I shall confine therefore my following discourse only to such as
challenge the repute of wisdom, and seemingly pass

for men of the soundest intellectuals.* Among
whom the Grammarians present themselves in the
front, a sort of men who would be the most miserable, the most slavish, and the most hateful of all
persons, if I did not in some way alleviate the press-
ures and miseries of their profession by blessing
them with a bewitching sort of madness: for they
are not only liable to those five curses, which they
so oft recite from the first five verses of Homer, but
to five hundred more of a worse nature; as always
damned to thirst and hunger, to be choked with
dust in their unswept schools (schools, shall I term
them, or rather elaboratories, nay, bridewells, and
houses of correction?), to wear out themselves in
fret and drudgery; to be deafened with the noise of
gaping boys; and in short, to be stifled with heat
and stench; and yet they cheerfully put up with all
these inconveniences, and, by the help of a fond conceit, think themselves as happy as any men living:
taking a great pride and delight in frowning and
looking big upon the trembling urchins, in boxing,
slashing, striking with the ferula, and in the exercise
of all their other methods of tyranny; while thus
lording it over a parcel of young, weak chits, they
imitate the Cuman ass,† and think themselves as
stately as a lion, that domineers over all the inferior
herd. Elevated with this conceit, they can hold filth
and nastiness to be an ornament; can reconcile their
nose to the most intolerable smells; and finally, think

*"Eos qui .   .   aureum illum ramum, ut aiunt, aucupantur,"
says Erasmus, alluding to the story of Eneas and the golden bough in
Vergil.   †Which got into the lion's skin.

*"Take a great pride and delight
in . . . boxing, slashing, striking
with the ferula"*

their wretched slavery the most arbitrary kingdom, which they would not exchange for the jurisdiction of Phalaris or Dionysius: and they are yet more happy by a strong persuasion of their own parts and abilities; for thus when their employment is only to rehearse silly stories, and poetical fictions, they will yet think themselves wiser than the best experienced philosopher; nay, they have an art of making ordinary people, such as their schoolboys' fond parents, to think them as considerable as their own pride has made them. Add hereunto this other sort of ravishing pleasure: when any of them has found out who was the mother of Anchises, or has lighted upon some old unusual word, such as *bubsequa, bovinator, manticulator,* or other like obsolete cramp terms; or can, after a great deal of poring, spell out the inscription of some battered monument; Lord! what joy, what triumph, what congratulating their success, as if they had conquered Africa, or taken Babylon the Great! When they recite some of their frothy, bombast verses, if any happen to admire them, they are presently flushed with the least hint of commendation, and devoutly thank Pythagoras for his grateful hypothesis, whereby they are now become actuated with a descent of Vergil's poetic soul. Nor is any diversion more pleasant, than when they meet to flatter and curry one another; yet they are so critical, that if any one hap to be guilty of the least slip, or seeming blunder, another shall presently correct him for it, and then to it they go in a tongue-combat, with all the fervour, spleen, and eagerness imaginable. May Priscian himself be my enemy if what I am now going to say be not exactly true. I knew an old Sophister that was a Grecian, a Latinist, a mathematician, a philosopher, a musician, and all to the utmost perfection, who after threescore years' experience in the world, had spent the last twenty of them only in drudging to conquer the criticisms of grammar, and made it the chief part of his prayers, that his life might be so long spared till he had learned how rightly to distinguish betwixt the eight parts of speech, which no grammarian, whether Greek or Latin, had yet accurately done. If any chance to have placed that as a conjunction which ought to have been used as an adverb, it is a sufficient alarm to raise a war for doing justice to the injured word. And since there have been as many several grammars, as particular grammarians (nay, more, for Aldus alone wrote five distinct grammars for his own share), the schoolmaster must be obliged to consult them all, sparing for no time nor trouble, though never so great, lest he should be otherwise posed in an unobserved criticism, and so by an irreparable disgrace lose the reward of all his toil. It is indifferent to me whether you call this folly or madness, since you must needs confess that it is by my influence these school-tyrants, though in never so despicable a condition, are so happy in their own thoughts, that they would not change fortunes with the most illustrious Sophi of Persia.

The Poets, although somewhat less beholden to

*"Those scribbling fops who
. . . set up for authors."*

me, are yet avowedly of my faction, being a sort of lawless blades, as the Grecian proverb says, the whole intent of whose profession is only to smooth up and tickle the ears of fools, by mere toys and fabulous shams, with which (however ridiculous) they are so bolstered up in an airy imagination, as to promise themselves an everlasting name, and promise, by their balderdash, at the same time to celebrate the never-dying memory of others. To these rapturous wits self-love and flattery are never-failing attendants; nor do any prove more zealous or constant devotees to folly.

The Rhetoricians likewise, though they are ambitious of being ranked among the Philosophers, yet are apparently of my faction, as appears among other arguments, by this more especially: in that among their several topics of completing the art of oratory, they all particularly insist upon the knack of jesting, which is one species of folly; as is evident from the books of oratory dedicated to Herennius, put among Cicero's work, but done by some other unknown author; and in Quintilian, that great master of eloquence, there is one large chapter spent in prescribing the methods of raising laughter: in short, they may well attribute a great efficacy to folly, since on any argument they can many times by a subterfuge laugh over what they could never seriously confute.

Of the same gang are those scribbling fops, who think to eternize their memory by setting up for authors: among which, though they are all some way indebted to me, yet are those more especially so, who spoil paper in blotting it with mere trifles and impertinences. For as to those graver drudgers to the press, that write learnedly, beyond the reach of an ordinary reader, who durst submit their labours to the review of the most severe critic, these are not so liable to be envied for their honour, as to be pitied for their sweat, and slavery. They make additions, alterations, blot out, write anew, amend, interline, turn it upside down, and yet can never please their fickle judgment, but that they shall dislike the next hour what they penned the former; and all this to purchase the airy commendations of a few understanding readers, which at most is but a poor reward for all their fastings, watchings, confinements, and brain-breaking tortures of invention. Add to this the impairing of their health, the weakening of their constitution, their contracting sore eyes, or perhaps turning stark blind; their poverty, their envy, their debarment from all pleasures, their hastening on old age, their untimely death, and what other inconveniences of a like or worse nature can be thought upon: and yet the recompense for all this severe penance is at best no more than a mouthful or two of frothy praise. These, as they are more laborious, so are they less happy than those other hackney scribblers which I first mentioned, who never stand much to consider, but write what comes next at a venture, knowing that the more silly their compositions are, the more they will be bought up by the greater number of readers, who are fools and blockheads: and if they hap to be condemned by

*"Their names are embossed
. . . upon the title-page."*

some few judicious persons, it is an easy matter by
clamour to drown their censure, and to silence them
by urging the more numerous commendations of
others. They are yet the wisest who transcribe
whole discourses from others, and then reprint them
as their own. By doing so they make a cheap and
easy seizure to themselves of that reputation which
cost the first author so much time and trouble to
procure. If they are at any time pricked a little in
conscience for fear of discovery, they feed themselves however with this hope, that if they be at last
found plagiaries, yet at least for some time they will
have had the credit of passing for the genuine authors. It is pleasant to see how all these several
writers are puffed up with the least blast of applause,
especially if they come to the honour of being pointed at as they walk along the streets, when their
several pieces are laid open upon every bookseller's
stall, when their names are embossed in a different
character upon the title-page, sometime only with the
two first letters, and sometime with fictitious cramp
terms, which few shall understand the meaning of;
and of those that do, all shall not agree in their verdict of the performance; some censuring, others ap-
proving it, men's judgments being as different as
their palates, that being toothsome to one which is
unsavoury and nauseous to another: though it is a
sneaking piece of cowardice for authors to put
feigned names to their works, as if, like bastards of
their brain, they were afraid to own them. Thus
one styles himself Telemachus, another Stelenus, or

Laertes, a third Polycrates, another Thrasymachus, and so on. By the same liberty we may ransack the whole alphabet, and jumble together any letters that come next to hand. It is farther very pleasant when these coxcombs employ their pens in writing congratulatory epistles, poems, and panegyricks, upon each other, wherein one shall be complimented with the title of Alcæus, another shall be charactered for the incomparable Callimachus; this shall be commended for a completer orator than Tully himself; a fourth shall be told by his fellow-fool that the divine Plato comes short of him for a philosophic soul. Sometime again they take up the cudgels, and challenge out an antagonist, and so get a name by a combat at dispute and controversy, while the unwary readers draw sides according to their different judgments: the longer the quarrel holds the more irreconcilable it grows; and when both parties are weary, they each pretend themselves the conquerors, and both lay claim to the credit of coming off with victory. These fooleries make sport for wise men, as being highly absurd, ridiculous and extravagant. True, but yet these paper-combatants, by my assistance, are so flushed with a conceit of their own greatness, that they prefer the solving of a syllogism before the sacking of Carthage; and upon the defeat of a poor objection carry themselves more triumphant than the most victorious Scipio.

Nay, even the learned and more judicious, that have wit enough to laugh at the others' folly, are very much beholden to my goodness; which (except ingratitude have drowned their ingenuousness) they must be ready upon all occasions to confess. Among these I suppose the lawyers will shuffle in for precedence, and they of all men have the greatest conceit of their own abilities. They will argue as confidently as if they spoke gospel instead of law; they will cite you six hundred several precedents, though not one of them come near to the case in hand; they will muster up the authority of judgments, deeds, glosses, and reports, and tumble over so many musty records, that they make their employ, though in itself easy, the greatest slavery imaginable; always accounting that the best plea which they have took most pains for.

To these, as bearing great resemblance to them, may be added logicians and sophisters, fellows that talk as much by rote as a parrot: who shall run down a whole gossiping of old women, nay, silence the very noise of a belfry, with louder clappers than those of the steeple; and if their unappeasable clamorousness were their only fault it would admit of some excuse; but they are at the same time so fierce and quarrelsome, that they will wrangle bloodily for the least trifle, and be so over intent and eager, that they many times lose their game in the chase and fright away that truth they are hunting for. Yet self-conceit makes these nimble disputants such doughty champions, that armed with three or four close-linked syllogisms, they shall enter the lists with the greatest masters of reason, and not question the foiling of them in an irresistible baffle: nay, their obstinacy makes them completely confident of their being in the right, though Stentor himself should shout against them.

Next to these come the philosophers in their long beards and short cloaks, who esteem themselves the only favourites of wisdom, and look upon the rest of mankind as the dirt and rubbish of the creation: yet these men's happiness is only a frantic craziness of brain; they build castles in the air, and infinite worlds in a *vacuum*. They will give you to a hair's breadth the dimensions of the sun, moon, and stars, as easily as they would do that of a flagon or pipkin: they will give a punctual account of the rise of thunder, of the origin of winds, of the nature of eclipses, and of all the other abstrusest difficulties in physics, without the least demur or hesitation, as if they had been admitted into the cabinet council of nature, or had been eye-witnesses to all the architecture of creation; though nature meantime laughs magnificently at all their conjectures; for they never yet made one considerable discovery, as appears in that they are unanimously agreed in no one point of the smallest moment; nothing so plain or evident but what by some or other is opposed and contradicted. But though they are ignorant of the artificial contexture of the least insect, they vaunt however, and brag that they know all things, when indeed they are unable to construe the mechanism of their own body; nay, when they are so purblind as not to be able to see a stone's cast before them, yet they shall be as sharp-sighted as possible in spying-out ideas,

The plague of being a heretic

universals, separate forms, first matters, quiddities, formalities, and a hundred such like niceties, so diminutively small, that were not their eyes extremely magnifying, all the art of optics could never make them discernible. But they then most despise the low grovelling vulgar when they bring out their parallels, triangles, circles, and other mathematical figures, drawn up in battalia, like so many spells and charms of conjuration in muster, with letters to refer to the explication of the several problems; hereby raising devils as it were, only to have the credit of laying them, and amusing the ordinary spectators into wonder, because they have not wit enough to understand the juggle. Of these some undertake to profess themselves judicial astrologers, pretending to keep correspondence with the stars, and so from their information can resolve any query; and though it is all but a presumptuous imposture, yet some to be sure will be so great fools as to believe them.

The divines present themselves next; but it may perhaps be most safe to pass them by, and not to touch upon so harsh a string as this subject would afford. Beside, the undertaking may be very hazardous; for they are a sort of men generally very hot and passionate: and should I provoke them, I doubt not would set upon me with a full cry, and force me with shame to recant, which if I stubbornly refuse to do, they will presently brand me for a heretic, and thunder out an excommunication, which is their spiritual weapon to wound such as lift up a hand against them. It is true, no men own a less dependence on me, yet have they reason to confess themselves indebted for no small obligations. For it is by one of my properties, self-love, that they fancy themselves, with their elder brother Paul, caught up into the third heaven, from whence, like shepherds indeed, they look down upon their flock, the laity, grazing, as it were, in the vales of the world below. They fence themselves in with so many surrounders of magisterial definitions, conclusions, corollaries, propositions explicit and implicit, that there is no falling in with them; or if they do chance to be urged to a seeming non-plus, yet they find out so many evasions, that all the art of man can never bind them so fast, but that an easy distinction shall give them a starting-hole to escape the scandal of being baffled. They will cut asunder the toughest argument with as much ease as Alexander did the Gordian knot; they will thunder out so many rattling terms as shall fright an adversary into conviction. They are exquisitely dexterous in unfolding the most intricate mysteries; they will tell you to a tittle all the successive proceedings of Omnipotence in the creation of the universe; they will explain the precise manner of original sin being derived from our first parents; they will satisfy you in what manner, by what degrees, and in how long a time, our Saviour was conceived in the Virgin's womb, and demonstrate in the consecrated wafer how accidents may subsist without a subject. Nay, these are accounted trivial, easy questions; they have yet far greater difficulties behind, which notwithstanding they solve with as much expedition as the former; as namely, whether supernatural generation requires any instant of time for its acting? whether Christ, as a son, bears a double specifically distinct relation to God the Father, and his virgin mother? whether this proposition is possible to be true, the first person of the Trinity hated the second? whether God, who took our nature upon him in the form of a man, could as well have become a woman, a devil, a beast, a herb, or a stone? and were it so possible that the Godhead had appeared in any shape of an inanimate substance, how he should then have preached his gospel, worked his miracles, or been nailed to the cross? whether if St. Peter had celebrated the eucharist at the same time our Saviour was hanging on the cross, the consecrated bread would have been transubstantiated into the same body that remained on the tree? whether in Christ's corporal presence in the sacramental wafer, his humanity be not abstracted from his Godhead? whether after the resurrection we shall carnally eat and drink as we do in this life? There are a thousand other more sublimated and refined niceties of notions, relations, quantities, formalities, quiddities, hæcceities, and such like abstrusities, as one would think no one could pry into, except he had not only such cat's eyes as to see best in the dark, but even such a piercing faculty as to see through an inch-board, and spy out what really never had any being. Add to these some of their tenets and opinions, which are so absurd and extravagant, that the wildest fancies of the Stoicks, which they so much disdain and decry as paradoxes, seem in comparison just and rational; as their maintaining, that it is a less aggravating fault to kill a hundred men, than for a poor cobbler to set a stitch on the Lord's day; or, that it is more justifiable to do the greatest injury imaginable to others, than to tell the least lie ourselves. And these subtleties are alchymized to a more refined sublimate by the abstracting brains of their several schoolmen; so that sooner should one escape the Labyrinth than the involutions of the Realists, the Nominalists, the Thomists, the Albertists, the Occamists, the Scotists. These are not all, but the rehearsal of a few only, as a specimen of their divided sects; in each of which there is so much of deep learning, so much of unfathomable difficulty, that I believe the apostles themselves would stand in need of a new illuminating spirit, if they were to engage in any controversy with these new divines. St. Paul, no question, had a full measure of faith; yet when he lays down faith to be the substance of things not seen, these men carp at it for an imperfect definition, and would undertake to teach the apostle better logic. Thus the same holy author wanted for nothing of the grace of charity, yet (say they) he describes and defines it but very inaccurately, when he treats of it in the thirteenth chapter of his first epistle to the Corinthians. The primitive disciples were very frequent in administering the holy sacrament, breaking bread from house to house; yet should they be asked of the *Terminus a quo* and the *Terminus ad quem;* the nature of transubstantiation; the manner how one body can be in several places at the same time; the difference betwixt the several attributes of Christ in heaven, on the cross. and in the consecrated bread; what time is required for the transubstantiating the bread into flesh; how it can be done by a short sentence pronounced by the priest, which sentence is a species of discrete quantity, that has no permanent *punctum:* were they asked (I say) these, and several other confused queries, I do not believe they could answer so readily as our mincing schoolmen nowadays take a pride to do. They were well acquainted with the mother of Jesus, yet none of them undertook to prove that she was preserved immaculate from the sin of Adam, as some of our divines very hotly contend for. St. Peter had the keys given to him, and that by our Saviour himself, who had never entrusted him except he had known him capable of their management and custody; and yet it is much to be questioned whether Peter was sensible of that subtlety broached by Scotus, that he may have the key of knowledge effectually for others, who has no knowledge actually in himself. Again, they baptized all nations, and yet never taught what was the formal, material, efficient. and final cause of baptism. and certainly never dreamt of distinguishing between a delible and an indelible character in this sacrament. They worshipped in the spirit. following their master's injunction. God is a spirit, and they which worship him, must worship him in spirit, and in truth; yet it does not appear that it was ever revealed to them how divine adoration should be paid at the same time to our blessed Saviour in heaven, and to his picture here below on a wall, drawn with two fingers held out, a bald crown, and a circle round his head. To reconcile these intricacies to an appearance of reason requires three-score years' experience in metaphysics.

Farther, the apostles often mention *Grace*, yet never distinguish between *gratia, gratis data,* and *gratia gratificans.* They earnestly exhort us likewise to good works, yet never explain the difference between *Opus operans,* and *Opus operatum.* They very frequently press and invite us to seek after charity, without dividing it into infused and acquired, or determining whether it be a substance or an accident, a created or an uncreated being. They detested sin themselves, and warned others from the commission of it; and yet I am sure they could never have defined it scientifically, unless they had been imbued with the spirit of the Scotists. St. Paul, who in others' judgment is no less the chief of the apostles, than he was in his own the chief of sinners, who being bred at the feet of Gamaliel, was certainly more eminently a scholar than any of the rest, yet he often exclaims against vain philosophy, warns us from doting about questions and strifes of words, and charges us to avoid profane and vain babblings, and oppositions of science falsely so

called; which he would not have done, if he had
thought it worth his while to have become acquainted with them, which he might soon have
been, the disputes of that age being but small, and
more intelligible sophisms, in reference to the vastly
greater intricacies they are now improved to.   But
yet, however, our scholastic divines are so modest,
that if they meet with any passage in St. Paul, or
any other penman of holy writ, which is not so
well modelled, or critically disposed of, as they
could wish, they will not roughly condemn it, but
bend it rather to a favorable interpretation, out of
reverence to antiquity, and partly through reverence
for the names of the apostles; though indeed it were
unreasonable to expect anything of this nature from
the apostles, whose lord and master had given unto
them to know the mysteries of God, but not those
of philosophy.   If the same divines meet with anything of like nature unpalatable in St. Chrysostom,
St. Basil, St. Hierom, or others of the fathers, they
will not stick to appeal from their authority, and
very fairly resolve that they lay under a mistake.
Yet these ancient fathers were they who confuted
both the Jews and the pagan philosophers, though
they both obstinately adhered to their respective
prejudices; they confuted them (I say), yet by their
lives and miracles, rather than by words and syllogisms; and the persons they thus proselyted were
downright honest, well meaning people, such as
understood plain sense better than any artificial
pomp of reasoning: whereas if our divines should

now set about the gaining converts from paganism by their metaphysical subtleties, they would find that most of the persons they applied themselves to were either so ignorant as not at all to apprehend them, or so impudent as to scoff and deride them; or finally, so well skilled at the same weapons, that they would be able to keep their pass, and fence off all assaults of conviction: and this last way the victory would be altogether as hopeless, as if two persons were engaged of so equal strength, that it were impossible any one should overpower the other.

If my judgment might be taken, I would advise Christians, in their next expedition to a holy war, instead of those many unsuccessful legions, which they have hitherto sent to encounter the Turks and Saracens, that they would furnish out their clamorous Scotists, their obstinate Occamists, their invincible Albertists, and all their forces of tough, crabbed and profound disputants: the engagement, I fancy, would be mighty pleasant, and the victory we may imagine on our side not to be questioned. For which of the enemies would not bow their turbans at so solemn an appearance? Which of the fiercest Janizaries would not throw away his scimitar, and all the half-moons be eclipsed by the interposition of so glorious an army?*

I suppose you mistrust I speak all this by way of jeer and irony; and well I may, since among

*"Totus hic locus εἰϱωνικῶς accipiendus." says the commentator. How reassuring to learn this!

divines themselves there are some so ingenious as
to despise these captious and frivolous impertinences: they look upon it as a kind of profane
sacrilege, and little less than a blasphemous im-
piety, to determine of such niceties in religion, as
ought rather to be the subject of an humble and
uncontradicting faith, than of a scrupulous and inquisitive reason: they abhor a defiling the mysteries
of Christianity with an intermixture of heathenish
philosophy, and judge it very improper to reduce
divinity to an obscure speculative science, whose
end is such a happiness as can be gained only by
the means of practice.   But alas, those notional
divines, however condemned by the soberer judgment of others, are yet mightily pleased with themselves, and are so laboriously intent upon prosecut-
ing their crabbed studies, that they cannot afford
so much time as to read a single chapter in any one
book of the whole Bible.   And while they thus
trifle away their mis-spent hours in trash and bab-
ble, they think that they support the Catholic
Church with the props and pillars of propositions
and syllogisms, no less effectually than Atlas is
feigned by the poets to sustain on his shoulders the
burden of a tottering world.   Their privileges, too,
and authority are very considerable: they can deal
with any text of scripture as with a nose of wax,
knead it into what shape best suits their interest;
and whatever conclusions they have dogmatically
resolved upon, they would have them as irrepeal-
ably ratified as Solon's laws, and in as great force

as the very decrees of the papal chair. If any be so bold as to remonstrate to their decisions, they will bring him on his knees to a recantation of his impudence. They shall pronounce as irrevocably as an oracle, 'This proposition is scandalous, that irreverent; this has a smack of heresy, and that is bald and improper.' So that it is not the being baptised into the church, the believing of the scriptures, the giving credit to St. Peter, St. Paul, St. Hierom, St. Augustin, nay, or St. Thomas Aquinas himself, that shall make a man a Christian, except he have the joint suffrage of these novices in learning, who have blessed the world no doubt with a great many discoveries, which had never come to light, if they had not struck the fire of subtlety out of the flint of obscurity. These fooleries sure must be a happy employ.

Farther, they make as many partitions and divisions in hell and purgatory, and describe as many different sorts and degrees of punishment as if they were very well acquainted with the soil and situation of those infernal regions. And to prepare a seat for the blessed above, they invent new orbs, and a stately empyrean heaven, so wide and spacious as if they had purposely contrived it, that the glorified saints might have room enough to walk, to feast, or to take any recreation.

With these, and a thousand more such like toys, their heads are more stuffed and swelled than Jove, when he went big of Pallas in his brain, and was forced to use the midwifery of Vulcan's axe to ease

him of his teeming burden. Do not wonder, therefore, that at public disputations they bind their
heads with so many caps one over another; for this
is to prevent the loss of their brains, which would
otherwise break out from their uneasy confinement.
It affords likewise a pleasant scene of laughter, to
listen to these divines in their hotly managed disputations; to see how proud they are of talking
such hard gibberish, and stammering out such
blundering distinctions, as the auditors perhaps may
sometimes gape at, but seldom apprehend: and they
take such a liberty in their speaking of Latin, that
they scorn to stick at the exactness of syntax or
concord; pretending it is below the majesty of a
divine to talk like a pedagogue, and be tied to the
slavish observance of the rules of grammar. Finally, they take a vast pride, among other citations,
to allege the authority of their respective master,
which word they bear as profound a respect to as
the Jews did to their ineffable *tetragrammaton,**
and therefore they will be sure never to write it
any otherwise than in great letters, MAGISTER
NOSTER; and if any happen to invert the order
of the words, and say, *noster magister,* they will
presently exclaim against him as a pestilent heretic
and underminer of the Catholic faith.

The next to these are another sort of brain-sick
fools, who style themselves monks and of religious
orders, though they assume both titles very un-
justly: for as to the last, they have very little re-

*The four Hebrew letters that represented the name of Yahwe.

ligion in them; and as to the former, the etymology
of the word monk implies a solitariness, or being
alone; whereas they are so thick abroad that we
cannot pass any street or alley without meeting
them. Now I cannot imagine what one degree of
men would be more hopelessly wretched, if I did
not stand their friend, and buoy them up in that
lake of misery, which by the engagements of a holy
vow they have voluntarily immerged themselves in.
But when men of this sort are so unwelcome to
others, as that the very sight of them is thought
ominous, I yet make them highly in love with themselves, and fond admirers of their own happiness.
The first step whereunto they esteem a profound
ignorance, thinking carnal knowledge a great enemy
to their spiritual welfare, and seem confident of
becoming the greater proficients in divine mysteries,
the less they are poisoned with any human learning.
They imagine that they bear a sweet consort with
the heavenly choir, when they tone out their daily
tally of psalms, which they rehearse only by rote,
without permitting their understanding or affections to go along with their voice. Among these
some make a good profitable trade of beggary,
going about from house to house, not like the
apostles, to break, but to beg, their bread; nay,
thrust into all public-houses, come aboard the pass-
age-boats, get into the travelling waggons, and
omit no opportunity of time or place for the crav-
ing people's charity; doing a great deal of injury
to common highway beggars by interloping in their

*"Highly in love with them-
selves, and fond admirers of their
own happiness"*

traffic of alms. And when they are thus voluntarily poor, destitute, not provided with two coats, nor with any money in their purse, they have the impudence to pretend that they imitate the first disciples, whom their master expressly sent out in such an equipage. It is pretty to observe how they regulate all their actions as it were by weight and measure to so exact a proportion, as if the whole loss of their religion depended upon the omission of the least punctilio. Thus they must be very critical in the precise number of knots to the tying on of their sandals; what distinct colours their respective habits, and what stuff made of; how broad and long their girdles; how big, and in what fashion, their hoods; whether their bald crowns be to a hair's-breadth of the right cut; how many hours they must sleep, at what minute rise to prayers, &c. And these several customs are altered according to the humours of different persons and places. While they are sworn to the superstitious observance of these trifles, they do not only despise all others, but are very inclinable to fall out among themselves; for though they make profession of an apostolic charity, yet they will pick a quarrel, and be implacably passionate for such poor provocations, as the girting on a coat the wrong way, or the wearing of clothes a little too darkish coloured, or any such nicety not worth the speaking of. Some are so obstinately superstitious that they will wear their upper garment of some coarse dog's hair stuff, and that next their skin as soft as silk: but others on the contrary will have linen frocks outermost, and their shirts of wool, or hair. Some again will abhor touching money as though it were as poisonous as aconite, though they make no scruple of the sin of drunkenness, and the lust of the flesh. All their several orders are mindful of nothing more than of their being distinguished from each other by their different customs and habits. They seem indeed not so careful of becoming like Christ, and of being known to be his disciples, as the being unlike to one another, and distinguishable for followers of their several founders. A great part of their religion consists in their title: some will be called cordeliers, and these subdivided into capuchines, minors, minims, and mendicants; some again are styled Benedictines, others of the order of St. Bernard, others of that of St. Bridget; some are Augustin monks, some Willielmites, and others Jacobists, as if the common name of Christian were too mean and vulgar. Most of them place their greatest stress for salvation on a strict conformity to their foppish ceremonies, and a belief of their legendary traditions; wherein they fancy to have acquitted themselves with so much of supererogation, that one heaven can never be a condign reward for their meritorious life: little thinking that the Judge of all the earth at the last day shall put them off, with a 'Who hath required these things at your hands?' and call them to account only for the stewardship of his legacy, which was the precept of love and charity. It will be pretty to hear their pleas before the great tribunal: one will brag how he mortified his carnal appetite by feeding only upon fish: another will urge that he spent most of his time on earth in the divine exercise of singing psalms: a third will tell how many days he fasted, and what severe penance he imposed on himself for the bringing his body into subjection: another shall produce in his own behalf as many ceremonies as would load a fleet of merchant-men: a fifth shall plead that in threescore years he never so much as touched a piece of money, except he fingered it through a thick pair of gloves: a sixth, to testify his former humility, shall bring along with him his sacred hood, so old and nasty, that any seaman had rather stand bare headed on the deck than put it on to defend his ears in the sharpest storms: the next that comes to answer for himself shall plead, that for fifty years together, he had lived like a sponge upon the same place, and was content never to change his homely habitation: another shall whisper softly, and tell the judge he has lost his voice by a continual singing of holy hymns and anthems: the next shall confess how he fell into a lethargy by a strict, reserved, and sedentary life: and the last shall intimate that he has forgot to speak, by having always kept silence, in obedience to the injunction of taking heed lest he should have offended with his tongue.   But amidst all their fine excuses our Saviour shall interrupt them with this answer, Woe unto you, scribes and pharisees, hypocrites, verily I know you not; I left you but one precept, of loving one another, which I do not hear any one plead he has faithfully discharged: I told you plainly in my gospel, without any parable, that my father's kingdom was prepared not for such as should lay claim to it by austerities, prayers, or fastings, but for those who should render themselves worthy of it by the exercise of faith, and the offices of charity: I cannot own such as depend on their own merits without a reliance on my mercy: as many of you therefore as trust to the broken reeds of your own deserts may even go search out a new heaven, for you shall never enter into that, which from the foundations of the world was prepared only for such as are true of heart. When these monks and friars shall meet with such a shameful repulse, and see that ploughmen and mechanics are admitted into that kingdom, from which they themselves are shut out, how sneakingly will they look, and how pitifully slink away? Yet till this last trial they had more comfort of a future happiness, because more hopes of it than any other men. And these persons are not only great in their own eyes, but highly esteemed and respected by others, especially those of the order of mendicants, whom none dare to offer any affront to, because as confessors they are intrusted with all the secrets of particular intrigues, which they are bound by oath not to discover; yet many times, when they are almost drunk, they cannot keep their tongue so far within their head, as not to be babbling out some hints, and shewing themselves so full, that they are in pain to be delivered. If any person give them the least provocation they will sure to be revenged of him, and in their next public harangue give him such shrewd wipes and reflections, that the whole congregation must needs take notice at whom they are levelled; nor will they ever desist from this way of declaiming, till their mouth be stopped with a bribe to hold their tongue. All their preaching is mere stage-playing, and their delivery the very transports of ridicule and drollery. Good Lord! how mimical are their gestures? What heights and falls in their voice? What toning, what bawling, what singing, what squeaking, what grimaces, making of mouths, apes' faces, and distorting of their countenance; and this art of oratory as a choice mystery, they convey down by tradition to one another. The manner of it I may adventure thus farther to enlarge upon. First, in a kind of mockery they implore the divine assistance, which they borrowed from the solemn custom of the poets: then if their text suppose be of charity, they shall take their exordium as far off as from a description of the river Nile in Egypt; or if they are to discourse of the mystery of the Cross, they shall begin from Babylon with the story of Bel and the Dragon; or perchance if their subject be of fasting, for an entrance to their sermon they shall pass through the twelve signs of the zodiac; or lastly, if they are to preach of faith, they shall address themselves in a long mathematical account of the squaring of the circle. I myself once heard a great fool (a great scholar, I should have said) undertaking in a laborious discourse to explain the mystery of the Holy Trinity; in the unfolding whereof, that he might shew his wit and reading, and together satisfy itching ears, he proceeded in a new method, as by insisting on the letters, syllables, and proposition, on the concord of noun and verb, and that of noun substantive, and noun adjective; the auditors all wondered, and some mumbled to themselves that hemistich of Horace,

Why all this needless trash?

But at last he brought it thus far, that he could demonstrate the whole Trinity to be represented by these first rudiments of grammar, as clearly and plainly as it was possible for a mathematician to draw a triangle in the sand; and for the making of this grand discovery, this subtle divine had sweated so hard for eight months together, that he studied himself as blind as a beetle, the intenseness of the eye of his understanding overshadowing and extinguishing that of his body; and yet he did not at all repent him of his blindness, but thinks the loss of his sight an easy purchase for the gain of glory and credit.

I heard at another time a grave divine, of fourscore years of age at least, so sour and hard-favoured, that one would be apt to mistrust that it was Scotus Redivivus; he taking upon him to treat of the mysterious name, JESUS, did very subtly pretend that in the very letters was contained, whatever could be said of it: for first, its being declined

only with three cases, did expressly point out the
trinity of persons. Then that the nominative
ended in S, the accusative in M, and the ablative
in U, did imply some unspeakable mystery, viz.,
that in words of those initial letters Christ was the
summus, or beginning, the *medius*, or middle, and
the *ultimus*, or end of all things. There was yet a
more abstruse riddle to be explained, which was by
dividing the word JESUS into two parts, and separating the S in the middle from the two extreme
syllables, making a kind of pentameter, the word
consisting of five letters: and this intermedial S
being in the Hebrew alphabet called sin, which in
the English language signifies what the Latins term
peccatum, was urged to imply that the holy Jesus
should purify us from all sin and wickedness. Thus
did the pulpiteer cant, while all the congregation,
especially the brotherhood of divines, were so surprised at his odd way of preaching, that wonder
served them, as grief did Niobe: it almost turned
them into stones. I among the rest (as Horace describes Priapus viewing the enchantments of the two
sorceresses, Canidia and Sagane) could no longer
contain, but let fly a cracking report of the operation it had upon me. √These impertinent introduc-
tions are not without reason condemned; for of
old, whenever Demosthenes among the Greeks, or
Tully among the Latins, began their orations with
so great a digression from the matter in hand, it was
always looked upon as improper and unelegant, and
indeed, were such a long-fetched exordium any

token of a good invention, shepherds and ploughmen might lay claim to the title of men of greatest
parts, since upon any argument it is easiest for them
to talk what is least to the purpose. √These preachers think their preamble (as we may well term it)
to be the most fashionable, when it is farthest from
the subject they propose to treat of, while each audi-
tor sits and wonders what they drive at, and many
times mutters out the complaint of Vergil:—

Whither does all this jargon tend?

In the third place, when they come to the division
of their text, they shall give only a very short
touch at the interpretation of the words, when
the fuller explication of their sense ought to have
been their only province. Fourthly, after they are
a little entered, they shall start some theological
queries, far enough off from the matter in hand,
and bandy them about pro and con till they lose
them in the heat of scuffle. And here they shall
cite their doctors invincible, subtle, seraphic, cher-
ubic, holy, irrefragable, and such like great names
to confirm their several assertions. Then out they
bring their syllogisms, their majors, their minors,
conclusions, corollaries, suppositions, and distinctions, that will sooner terrify the congregation into
an amazement, than persuade them into a conviction. √Now comes the fifth act, in which they must
exert their utmost skill to come off with applause.
Here therefore they fall a telling some sad lament-
able story out of their legend, or some other fabulous history, and this they descant upon allegori-

cally, tropologically, and anagogically; and so they draw to a conclusion of their discourse, which is a more brainsick chimera than ever Horace could describe in his *De Arte Poetica*, when he began:—
Humano Capiti, &c.

Their praying is altogether as ridiculous as their preaching; for imagining that in their addresses to heaven they should set out in a low and tremulous voice, as a token of dread and reverence, they begin therefore with such a soft whispering as if they were afraid any one should overhear what they said; but when they are gone a little way, they clear up their pipes by degrees, and at last bawl out so loud as if, with Baal's priests, they were resolved to awake a sleeping god; and then again, being told by rhetoricians that heights and falls, and a different cadence in pronunciation, are a great advantage to the setting off any thing that is spoken, they will sometimes as it were mutter their words inwardly, and then of a sudden hollo them out, and be sure to end in such a flat faltering tone as if their spirits were spent, and they had run themselves out of breath. ✓ Lastly, they have read that most systems of rhetoric treat of the art of exciting laughter; therefore for the effecting of this they will sprinkle some jests and puns that must pass for ingenuity, though they are only the froth and folly of affectedness. Sometimes they will nibble at the wit of being satyrical, though their utmost spleen is so toothless, that they suck rather than bite, tickle rather than scratch or wound: nor do they ever flatter more than at such times as they pretend to speak with greatest freedom.

Finally, all their actions are so buffoonish and mimical, that any would judge they had learned all their tricks of mountebanks and stage-players, who in action it is true may perhaps outdo them, but in oratory there is so little odds between both, that it is hard to determine which seems of longest standing in the schools of eloquence. Yet these preachers, however ridiculous, meet with such hearers, who admire them as much as the people of Athens did Demosthenes, or the citizens of Rome could do Cicero: among which admirers are chiefly shopkeepers, and women, whose approbation and good opinion they only court; because the first, if they are humoured, give them some snacks out of unjust gain; and the last come and ease their grief to them upon all pinching occasions. especially when their husbands are any ways cross or unkind.*

Thus much I suppose may suffice to make you sensible how much these cell-hermits and recluses are indebted to my bounty; who when they tyrannize over the consciences of the deluded laity with fopperies, juggles, and impostures, yet think themselves as eminently pious as St. Paul, St. Anthony, or any other of the saints; but these stage-divines, not less ungrateful disowners of their obligations to Folly, than they are impudent pretenders to the profession of piety, I willingly take my leave of, and pass now to kings, princes, and courtiers, who

*Cf. the remarks in the Introduction on Erasmus' attitude toward the monks, and their hatred of him.

paying me a devout acknowledgment, may justly
challenge back the respect of being mentioned and
taken notice of by me. And first, had they wisdom
enough to make a true judgment of things, they
would find their own condition to be more despicable and slavish than that of the most menial
subjects. For certainly none can esteem perjury
or parricide a cheap purchase for a crown, if he does
but seriously reflect on that weight of cares a prince-
ly diadem is loaded with. He that sits at the helm
of government acts in a public capacity, and so
must sacrifice all private interest to the attainment
of the common good; he must himself be conformable to those laws his prerogative exacts, or else he
can expect no obedience paid them from others; he
must have a strict eye over all his inferior magistrates and officers, or otherwise it is to be doubted
they will but carelessly discharge their respective
duties. Every king, within his own territories, is
placed for a shining example as it were in the firma-
ment of his wide-spread dominions, to prove either
a glorious star of benign influence, if his behaviour
be remarkably just and innocent, or else to impend
as a threatening comet, if his blazing power be pestilent and hurtful. Subjects move in a darker
sphere, and so their wanderings and failings are less
discernible; whereas princes, being fixed in a more
exalted orb, and encompassed with a brighter dazz-
ling lustre, their spots are more apparently visible,
and their eclipses, or other defects, influential on
all that is inferior to them. Kings are baited with

so many temptations and opportunities to vice and immorality, such as are high feeding, liberty, flattery, luxury, and the like, that they must stand perpetually on their guard, to fence off those assaults that are always ready to be made upon them. In fine, abating from treachery, hatred, dangers, fear, and a thousand other mischiefs impending on crowned heads, however uncontrollable they are this side heaven, yet after their reign here they must appear before a supremer judge, and there be called to an exact account for the discharge of that great stewardship which was committed to their trust. If princes did but seriously consider (and consider they would if they were but wise) these many hardships of a royal life, they would be so perplexed in the result of their thoughts thereupon, as scarce to eat or sleep in quiet. But now by my assistance they leave all these cares to the gods, and mind only their own ease and pleasure, and therefore will admit none to their attendance but who will divert them with sport and mirth, lest they should otherwise be seized and damped with the surprisal of sober thoughts. They think they have sufficiently acquitted themselves in the duty of governing, if they do but ride constantly a-hunting, breed up good race-horses, sell places and offices to those of their courtiers that will give most for them, and find out new ways for invading of their people's property, and hooking in a larger revenue to their own exchequer; for the procurement whereof they will always have some pretended claim and title; that

though it be manifest extortion, yet it may bear
the show of law and justice: and then they daub
over their oppression with a submissive, flattering
carriage, that they may so far insinuate into the
affections of the vulgar, as they may not tumult nor
rebel, but patiently crouch to burdens and exac-
tions.* Let us feign now a person ignorant of the
laws and constitutions of that realm he lives in,
an enemy to the public good, studious only for his
own private interest, addicted wholly to pleasures
and delights, a hater of learning, a professed enemy
to liberty and truth, careless and unmindful of the
common concerns, taking all the measures of justice and honesty from the false beam of self-interest
and advantage; after this hang about his neck a
gold chain, for an intimation that he ought to have
all virtues linked together; then set a crown of gold
and jewels on his head, for a token that he ought to
overtop and outshine others in all commendable
qualifications; next, put into his hand a royal scep-
tre for a symbol of justice and integrity; lastly,
clothe him with purple, for an hieroglyphic of a
tender love and affection to the commonwealth.   If
a prince should look upon this portraiture, and draw
a comparison between that and himself, certainly

*After reading this account of the kings and lawmakers of four
centuries ago, let us duly congratulate ourselves on the complete purifi-
cation of government and politics which has happily been achieved in our
glorious Republic, where no such scandals or extortions can possibly
occur, and where no lawmaker would ever dream of disobeying any law
he had helped to impose upon others. Especially must we felicitate ourselves upon the entire success of the XVIII Amendment and the Volstead
law, both so religiously and scrupulously observed by all our politicians,
law-makers and officials. How great is our advance since the days of
Erasmus. Selab!

he would be ashamed of his ensigns of majesty, and be afraid of being laughed out of them.

Next to kings themselves may come their courtiers, who, though they are for the most part a base, servile, cringing, low-spirited sort of flatterers, yet they look big, swell great, and have high thoughts of their honour and grandeur. Their confidence appears upon all occasions; yet in this one thing they are very modest, in that they are content to adorn their bodies with gold, jewels, purple, and other glorious ensigns of virtue and wisdom, but leave their minds empty and unfraught; and taking the resemblance of goodness to themselves, turn over the truth and reality of it to others. They think themselves mighty happy in that they can call the king master, and be allowed the familiarity of talking with him; that they can volubly rehearse his several titles of August Highness, Supereminent Excellence, and Most Serene Majesty; that they can boldly usher in any discourse, and that they have the complete knack of insinuation and flattery; for these are the arts that make them truly genteel and noble. · If you make a stricter enquiry after their other endowments, you shall find them mere sots and dolts. They will sleep generally till noon, and then their mercenary chaplains shall come to their bed-side, and entertain them perhaps with a short morning prayer. As soon as they are drest they must go to breakfast, and when that is done, immediately to dinner. When the cloth is taken away, then to cards, dice, tables, or some such

"Look big, swell great, and have high thoughts of their honour and grandeur"

like diversion. After this they must have one or two afternoon banquets, and so in the evening to supper. When they have supped, then begins the game of drinking; the bottles are marshalled, the glasses ranked, and round go the healths and bumpers till they are carried to bed. And this is the constant method of passing away their hours, days, months, years, and ages. I have many times taken great satisfaction by standing in the court, and seeing how the tawdry butterflies vie upon one another: the ladies shall measure the height of their honours by the length of their trails, which must be borne up by a page behind. The nobles jostle one another to get nearest to the king's elbow, and wear gold chains of that weight and bigness as require no less strength to carry than they do wealth to purchase.

And now for some reflections upon popes, cardinals, and bishops, who in pomp and splendour have almost equalled if not outgone secular princes. Now if any one consider that their upper crotchet of white linen is to signify their unspotted purity and innocence; that their forked mitres, with both divisions tied together by the same knot, are to denote the joint knowledge of the Old and New Testament; that their always wearing gloves, represents their keeping their hands clean and undefiled from lucre and covetousness; that the pastoral staff implies the care of a flock committed to their charge; that the cross carried before them expresses their victory over all carnal affections; he (I say) that considers this, and much more of the like nature, must needs conclude they are entrusted with a very weighty and difficult office. But now, they think it sufficient if they can but feed themselves; and as to their flock, either commend them to the care of Christ himself, or commit them to the guidance of some inferior vicars and curates; not so much as remembering what their name of bishop imports, to wit, labour, pains, and diligence, but by base simoniacal contracts, they are in a profane sense *Episcopi, i.e.,* overseers of their own gain and income.*

So cardinals, in like manner, if they did but consider that the Church supposes them to succeed in the room of the apostles; that therefore they must behave themselves as their predecessors, and so not be lords, but dispensers of spiritual gifts, of the disposal whereof they must one day render a strict account: or if they would but reflect a little on their habit, and thus reason with themselves: what means this white upper garment, but only an unspotted innocence? What signifies my inner purple, but only an ardent love and zeal to God? What imports my outermost pall, so wide and long that it covers the whole mule when I ride, nay, should be big enough to cover a camel, but only a diffusive charity, that should spread itself for a succour and protection to all, by teaching, exhorting, comforting, reproving, admonishing, composing of

---

* «Ἐπισχοπεῖν», the accurate Listrius reminds us, "est inspicere, et curam agere, prospicereque de necessariis; et ἐπίσχοπος est inspector et curator." The reminder was probably more necessary before the Reformation than since.

"They are content to adorn their bodies."

differences, courageously withstanding wicked princes, and sacrificing for the safety of our flock our life and blood, as well as our wealth and riches; though indeed riches ought not to be at all possessed by such as boast themselves successors to the apostles, who were poor, needy, and destitute: √I say, if they did but lay these considerations to heart they would never be so ambitious of being created to this honour, they would willingly resign it when conferred upon them, or at least would be as industrious, watchful and laborious, as the primitive apostles were.

Now as to the popes of Rome, who pretend themselves Christ's vicars, if they would but imitate his exemplary life,* in the being employed in an unintermitted course of preaching; in the being attended with poverty, nakedness, hunger, and a contempt of this world; if they did but consider the import of the word pope, which signifies a father; or if they did but practice their cognomen of most holy, what order or degrees of men would be in a worse condition? /There would be then no such vigorous making of parties, and buying of votes, in the conclave upon a vacancy of that see: and those who by bribery, or other indirect courses, should get themselves elected, would never secure their sitting firm in the chair by pistol, poison, force, and viol-

---

*That was the trouble with Erasmus: he always wanted people to *live* their religion, instead of swaggering about the orthodoxy of their belief. The idea of telling cardinals they ought to live like the Apostles, and the Vicar of Christ that he ought to suggest his Chief to people, instead of being the head of the biggest political machine in the world! No wonder the machine placed Erasmus' books on the Index.

ence. How much of their pleasure would be abated
if they were but endowed with one dram of wisdom? Wisdom, did I say? Nay, with one grain
of that salt which our Saviour bid them not lose
the savour of. All their riches, all their honour,
their jurisdictions, their Peter's patrimony, their
offices, their dispensations, their licenses, their indulgences, their long train and attendants (see in
how short a compass I have abbreviated all their
marketing of religion); in a word, all their perquisites would be forfeited and lost; and in their
room would succeed watchings, fastings, tears, prayers, sermons, hard studies, repenting sighs, and a
thousand such like severe penalties: nay, what's
yet more deplorable, it would then follow, that all
their clerks, amanuenses, notaries, advocates, proc-
tors, secretaries, the offices of grooms, ostlers, serving-men, pimps (and somewhat else, which for
modesty's sake I shall not mention); in short, all
these troops of attendants, which depend on His
Holiness, would all lose their several employments.
This indeed would be hard, but what yet remains
would be more dreadful: the very Head of the
Church, the spiritual prince, would then be brought
from all his splendour to the poor equipage of a
scrip and staff. But all this is upon the supposition
only that they understood what circumstances they
are placed in; whereas now, by a wholesome neglect
of thinking, they live as well as heart can wish.
Whatever of toil and drudgery belongs to their office
that they assign over to St. Peter, or St. Paul, who

*"The Popes of Rome, who pre-
tend themselves Christ's vicars"*

have time enough to mind it; but if there be any
thing of pleasure and grandeur, that they assume
to themselves, as being hereunto called: so that by
my influence no sort of people live more to their
own ease and content. They think to satisfy that
Master they pretend to serve, our Lord and Saviour,
with their great state and magnificence, with the
ceremonies of instalments, with the titles of reverence and holiness, and with exercising their episcopal
function only in blessing and cursing. The work-
ing of miracles is old and out-moded; to teach the
people is too laborious; to interpret scripture is to
invade the prerogative of the schoolmen; to pray
is too idle; to shed tears is cowardly and unmanly;
to fast is too mean and sordid; to be easy and familiar is beneath the grandeur of him, who, without
being sued to and intreated, will scarce give princes
the honour of kissing his toe; finally to die for religion is too self-denying; and to be crucified like
their Lord, is base and ignominious. Their only
weapons ought to be those of the Spirit; and of
these indeed they are mighty liberal, as of their
interdicts, their suspensions, their denunciations,
their aggravations, their greater and lesser excom-
munications, and their roaring bulls, that fright
whomever they are thundered against; and these
most holy fathers never issue them out more frequently than against those, who, at the instigation
of the devil, and not having the fear of God before
their eyes, do feloniously and maliciously attempt
to lessen and impair St. Peter's patrimony: and

though that apostle tells our Saviour in the gospel, in the name of all the other disciples. 'We have left all, and followed you,' yet they challenge as his inheritance, fields, towns, treasures, and large dominions; for the defending whereof, inflamed with a holy zeal, they fight with fire and sword, to the great loss and effusion of Christian blood, thinking they are apostolical maintainers of Christ's spouse, the Church, when they have murdered all such as they call her enemies; though indeed the Church has no enemies more bloody and tyrannical than such impious popes, who give dispensations for the not preaching of Christ; evacuate the main effect and design of our redemption by their pecuniary bribes and sales; adulterate the gospel by their forced interpretations, and undermining traditions; and lastly, by their lusts and wickedness grieve the Holy Spirit, and make their Saviour's wounds to bleed anew. Farther, when the Christian Church has been all along first planted, then confirmed, and since established by the blood of her martyrs, as if Christ her head would be wanting in the same methods still of protecting her, they invert the order, and propagate their religion now by arms and violence, which was wont formerly to be done only with patience and sufferings. And though war be so brutish, as that it becomes beasts rather than men; so extravagant, that the poets feigned it an effect of the furies; so licentious, that it stops the course of all justice and honesty; so desperate, that it is best waged by ruffians and banditti, and so un-

Monarchy, Jealousy, Clericalism
The three war-masters

christian, that it is contrary to the express commands of the gospel; yet maugre all this, peace is too quiet, too inactive, and they must be engaged in the boisterousness of war.   Among which undertaking popes, you shall have some so old that they can scarce creep, and yet they will put on a young, brisk resolution, will resolve to stick at no pains, to spare no cost, nor be deterred by any inconvenience, so they may involve laws, religion, peace, and all other concerns, whether sacred or civil, in unappeasable tumults and distractions.   And yet some of their learned fawning courtiers will interpret this notorious madness for zeal, and piety, and fortitude, having found out the way how a man may draw his sword, and sheathe it in his brother's bowels, and yet not offend against the duty of the second table, whereby we are obliged to love our neighbours as ourselves.   It is yet uncertain whether these Romish fathers have taken example from, or given precedent to, certain German bishops, who omitting their ecclesiastical habit, their cult, their benedictions, and other ceremonies, appear openly armed cap-a-pie, like so many champions and warriors, thinking no doubt that they come short of the duty of their function, if they die in any other place than the open field, fighting the battles of the

*It is scandalous to think such things should have been written about the saintly Alexander VI and the exemplary Julius II.   But we must remember that there was one excuse for Erasmus: the doctrine of papal infallibility had not in his day been invented.   Had he known that Alexander and Julius were infallible regarding faith and morals, he would doubtless have spoken of them with more becoming respect. Unluckily they did not know it themselves.

Lord. The inferior clergy, deeming it unmannerly
not to conform to their patrons and diocesans, devoutly tug and fight for their tithes with syllogisms
and arguments, as fiercely as with swords, sticks,
stones, or anything that came next to hand. When
they read the rabbis, fathers. or other ancient writings, how quick-sighted are they in spying out any
sentences, that they may frighten the people with,
and make them believe that more than the tenth is
due, passing by whatever they meet with in the same
authors that minds them of the duty and difficulty
of their own office. They never consider that their
shaven crown is a token that they should pare off
and cut away all the superfluous lusts of this world,
and give themselves wholly to divine meditation;
but instead of this, our bald-pated priests think they
have done enough, if they do but mumble over such
a fardel of prayers, which it is a wonder if God
should hear or understand, when they whisper them
so softly, and in so unknown a language, which they
can scarce hear or understand themselves. This
they have in common with other mechanics, that
they are most subtle in the craft of getting money,
and wonderfully skilled in their respective dues of
tithes, offerings, perquisites, &c. Thus they are all
content to reap the profit, but as to the burden, that
they toss as a ball from one hand to another, and
assign it over to any they can get or hire: for as secular princes have their judges and subordinate ministers to act in their name, and supply their stead; so
ecclesiastical governors have their deputies, vicars,

and curates, nay, many times turn over the whole
care of religion to the laity The laity, supposing they
have nothing to do with the Church (as if their
baptismal vow did not initiate them members of
it), make it over to the priests; of the priests again,
those that are secular, thinking their title implies
them to be a little too profane, assign this task over
to the regulars, the regulars to the monks; the monks
bandy it from one order to another, till it light upon
the mendicants; they lay it upon the Carthusians,
which order alone keeps honesty and piety among
them, but really keep them so close that no body
ever yet could see them.   Thus the Popes thrusting
only their sickle into the harvest of profit, leave all
the other toil of spiritual husbandry to the bishops,
the bishops bestow it upon the pastors, the pastors
on their curates, and the curates commit it to the
mendicants, who return it again to such as well
know how to make good advantage of the flock, by
the benefit of their fleece.

 But I would not be thought purposely to expose the weaknesses of popes and priests, lest I
should seem to recede from my title, and make a
satire instead of a panegyric: nor let anyone imagine
that I reflect on good princes, by commending of
bad ones: I did this only in brief, to shew that
there is no one particular person can lead a comfortable life, except he be entered of my society,
and retain me for his friend. Nor indeed can it be
otherwise, since fortune, that empress of the world,
is so much in league and amity with me, that to

wise men she is always stingy, and sparing of her gifts, but is profusely liberal and lavish to fools. Thus Timotheus, the Athenian commander, in all his expeditions, was a mirror of good luck, because he was a little underwitted; from him was occasioned the Grecian proverb, 'Η εΰδοντος κύρτος αἰρεῖ, *The net fills, though the fisherman sleeps;* there is also another favourable proverb, γλαὺξ ἵπταται, *The owl flies,* an omen of success. But against wise men are pointed these ill-boding proverbs, Ἐν τετράδι γεννηθέντας, *Born under a bad planet;* equum habet Seianum, *He cannot ride the fore horse;* aurum Tholosanum, *Ill-gotten goods will never prosper;* and more to the same purpose. But I forbear from any farther proverbializing, lest I should be thought to have rifled my Erasmus' adages. To return, therefore, fortune we find still favouring the blunt, and flushing the forward; strokes and smooths up fools, crowning all their undertakings with success; but wisdom makes her followers bashful, sneaking, and timorous, and therefore you see that they are commonly reduced to hard shifts, must grapple with poverty, cold and hunger, must lie recluse, despised, and unregarded, while fools roll in money, are advanced to dignities and offices, and in a word, have the whole world at command. If any one think it happy to be a favourite at court, and to manage the disposal of places and preferments, this happiness is so far from being attainable by wisdom, that the very suspicion of it would put a stop to all advancement. Has any man a mind to raise himself a good estate? What dealer in the world would ever get a farthing, if he be so wise as to scruple at perjury, blush at a lie, or stick at any fraud and over-reaching?

Farther, does any one appear a candidate for any ecclesiastical dignity? Why, an ass, or a plough-jobber, shall sooner gain it than a wise man. Again, are you in love with any handsome lady? Alas, women-kind are so addicted to folly, that they will not at all listen to the courtship of a wise suitor. Finally, wherever there is any preparation made for mirth and jollity, all wise men are sure to be excluded the company, lest they should stint the joy, and damp the frolic. In a word, to what side soever we turn ourselves, to popes, princes, judges, magistrates, friends, enemies, rich or poor, all their concerns are managed by money, which because it is undervalued by wise men, therefore, in revenge to be sure, it never comes at them.

But now, though my praise and commendation might well be endless, yet it is requisite I should put some period to my speech. I'll therefore draw toward an end, when I have first confirmed what I have said by authority of several authors. Which by way of farther proof I shall insist upon, partly, that I may not be thought to have said more in my own behalf than what will be justified by others; and partly, that the lawyers may not check me for citing no precedents nor allegations. To imitate them therefore I will produce some reports and authorities; though perhaps, like theirs too, they are nothing to the purpose.

First then, it is confessed almost to a proverb, that the art of dissembling is a very necessary accomplishment; and therefore it is a common verse among school-boys:

To feign the fool when fit occasions rise,
Argues the being more completely wise.

It is easy therefore to collect how great a value ought to be put upon real folly, when the very shadow, and bare imitation of it, is so much esteemed. Horace, who in his epistles thus styles himself:

My sleek-skinn'd corpse as smooth as if I lie
'Mong th' fatted swine of Epicurus' sty.

This poet (I say) gives this advice in one of his odes:

Short Folly with your counsels mix.

The epithet of short, it is true, is a little improper. The same poet again has this passage elsewhere:

Well-timed Folly has a sweet relish.

And in another place:

I'd rather much be censured for a fool,
Than feel the lash and smart of wisdom's school.

Homer praises Telemachus as much as any one of his heroes, and yet he gives him the epithet of νήπιος, *Silly*: and the Grecians generally use the same word to express children, as a token of their innocence. And what is the argument of all Homer's Iliads, but only, as Horace observes:

They kings' and subjects' dotages contain?

How positive also is Tully's commendation that all
places are filled with fools?   Now every excellence
being to be measured by its extent, the goodness of
Folly must be of as large compass as those universal
places she reaches to.   But perhaps Christians may
slight the authority of a heathen.   I could therefore, if I pleased, back and confirm the truth hereof
by the citation of several texts of scripture; though
herein it were perhaps my duty to beg leave of the
divines, that I might so far intrench upon their prerogative.   Supposing a grant, the task seems so
difficult as to require the invocation of some aid
and assistance; yet because it is unreasonable to put
the muses to the trouble and expense of so tedious
a journey, especially since the business is out of their
sphere, I shall choose rather (while I am acting the
divine, and venturing in their polemic difficulties),
to wish myself for such time animated with the
bristling and prickly soul of Scotus, which I would
not care how afterwards it returned to his body,
though for refinement it were stopped at a purgatory
by the way.   I cannot but wish that I might wholly
change my character, or at least that some grave
divine, in my stead, might rehearse this part of the
subject for me: for truly I suspect that somebody
will accuse me of plundering the closets of those
reverend men, while I pretend to so much divinity,
as must appear in my following discourse.   Yet
however, it may not seem strange, that after so
long and frequent a converse, I have gleaned some
scraps from the divines; since Horace's wooden god

by hearing his master read Homer, learned some
words of Greek; and Lucian's cock, by long attention, could readily understand what any man spoke.
But now to the purpose, wishing myself success.

Ecclesiastes doth somewhere confess that there
are an infinite number of fools. Now when he
speaks of an infinite number, what does he else but
imply, that herein is included the whole race of
mankind, except some very few, which I know not
whether ever any one had yet the happiness to see?

The prophet Jeremiah speaks yet more plainly
in his tenth chapter, where he saith, that *Every man
is brutish in his knowledge*. He just before attributes wisdom to God alone, saying, that the *Wise
men of the nations are altogether brutish and foolish*. And in the preceding chapter he gives this seasonable caution, *Let not the wise man glory in his
wisdom*: the reason is obvious, because no man hath
truly any whereof to glory. But to return to Ecclesiastes, when he saith, *Vanity of vanities, all is
vanity*, what else can we imagine his meaning to
be, than that our whole life is nothing but one continued interlude of Folly? This confirms that assertion of Tully, which is delivered in that noted
passage we but just now mentioned, namely, that
All places swarm with fools. Farther, what does
the son of Sirach mean when he saith in Ecclesiasti-
cus, that the *Fool is changed as the moon*, while
the *Wise man is fixed as the sun*, than only to hint
out the folly of all mankind; and that the name of
wise is due to no other but the all-wise God? for

all interpreters by Moon understand mankind, and
by Sun that fountain of all light, the Almighty.
The same sense is implied in that saying of our
Saviour in the gospel, *There is none good but one,
that is God:* for if whoever is not wise must be
consequently a fool, and if, according to the Stoicks,
every man be wise so far only as he is good, the meaning of the text must be, all mortals are unavoidably
fools; and there is none wise but one, that is God.
Solomon also in the fifteenth chapter of his Proverbs hath this expression, *Folly is joy to him that is
destitute of wisdom;* plainly intimating, that the
wise man is attended with grief and vexation, while
the foolish only roll in delight and pleasure.   To
the same purpose is that saying of his in the first
chapter of Ecclesiastes, *In much wisdom is much
grief; and he that increaseth knowledge increaseth
sorrow.*   Again, it is confessed by the same preacher
in the seventh chapter of the same book, *That the
heart of the wise is in the house of mourning, but
the heart of fools is in the house of mirth.*   This
author himself had never attained to such a portion
of wisdom, if he had not applied himself to a searching out the frailties and infirmities of human nature; as, if you believe not me, may appear from
his own words in his first chapter, *I gave my heart
to know wisdom, and to know madness and folly;*
where it is worthy to be observed that as to the
order of words, Folly for its advantage is put in
the last place.   Thus Ecclesiastes wrote, and thus
indeed did an ecclesiastical method require; namely,

that what has the precedence in dignity should
come hindmost in rank and order, according to the
tenor of that evangelical precept, *The last shall be
first, and the first shall be last.* And in Ecclesiasti-
cus likewise (whoever was author of the holy book
which bears that name) in the forty-fourth chapter,
the excellency of folly above wisdom is positively
acknowledged; the very words I shall not cite, till I
have the advantage of an answer to a question I am
proposing, this way of interrogating being frequently made use of by Plato in his dialogues between Socrates and other disputants: I ask you then, what is
it we usually hoard and lock up, things of greater
esteem and value, or those which are more common,
trite, and despicable? Why are you so backward in
making an answer? Since you are so shy and reserved, I'll take the Greek proverb for a satisfactory
reply; namely, τὴν ἐπὶ θύραις ὑδρίαν, *Foul water
is thrown down the sink;* which saying, that no
person may slight it, it may be convenient to ad-
vertise that it comes from no meaner an author than
that oracle of truth, Aristotle himself. And indeed
there is no one on this side Bedlam so mad as to
throw out upon the dunghill his gold and jewels,
but rather all persons have a close repository to preserve them in, and secure them under all the locks,
bolts and bars, that either art can contrive, or fears
suggest: whereas the dirt, pebbles, and oyster-shells,
that lie scattered in the streets, ye trample upon,
pass by, and take no notice of. If then what is
more valuable be coffered up, and what less so lies

unregarded, it follows, that accordingly Folly should meet with a greater esteem than wisdom, because that wise author advises us to the keeping close and concealing the first, and exposing or laying open the other: as take him now in his own words, *Better is he that hideth his folly than him that hideth his wisdom.* Beside, the sacred text does oft ascribe innocence and sincerity to fools, while the wise man is apt to be a haughty scorner of all such as he thinks or censures to have less wit than himself: 'for so I understand that passage in the tenth chapter of Ecclesiastes, *When he that is a fool walketh by the way, his wisdom faileth him, and he saith to every one that he is a fool.* Now what greater argument of candour or ingenuousness can there be, than to demean himself equal with all others, and not think their deserts any way inferior to his own?✓ Folly is no such scandalous attribute, but that the wise Agur was not ashamed to confess it, in the thirtieth chapter of Proverbs: *Surely I am more brutish than any man, and have not the understanding of a man.* Nay, St. Paul himself, that great doctor of the Gentiles, writing to his Corinthians, readily owns the name, saying, *If any man speak as a fool, I am more;* as if to have been less so had been a reproach and disgrace.

But perhaps I may be censured for mis-interpreting this text by some modern annotators, who, like crows pecking at one another's eyes, find fault, and correct all that went before them, pretend each their own glosses to contain the only true and genuine explication; among whom my Erasmus (whom I cannot but mention with respect) may challenge the second place, if not the precedency. This citation (say they) is purely impertinent; the meaning of the apostle is far different from what you dream of: he would not have these words so understood, as if he desired to be thought a greater fool than the rest, but only when he had before said, *Are they ministers of Christ?* so am *I:* as if the equalling himself herein to others had been too little, he adds, *I am more,* thinking a bare equality not enough, unless he were even superior to those he compares himself with. This he would have to be believed as true; yet lest it might be thought offensive, as bordering too much on arrogance and conceit, he tempers and alleviates it by the covert of Folly. *I speak* (says he) *as a fool,* knowing it to be the peculiar privilege of fools to speak the truth, without giving offence. But what St. Paul's thoughts were when he wrote this, I leave for them to determine. In my own judgment at least I prefer the opinion of the good old tun-bellied divines, with whom it's safer and more creditable to err, than to be in the right with smattering, raw novices.

Nor indeed should any one mind the late critics any more than the senseless chattering of a daw: especially since one of the most eminent of them (whose name I advisedly conceal, lest some of our wits should be taunting him with the Greek proverb, Ὄνος πρὸς λύραν, *ad lyram asinus*) magisterially and dogmatically descanting upon his text

[*are they the ministers of Christ?* (*I speak as a fool*)
I am more] makes a distinct chapter, and (which
without good store of logic he could never have
done) adds a new section, and then gives this paraphrase, which I shall verbatim recite, that you may
have his words materially, as well as formally his
sense (for that's one of their babbling distinctions).
[*I speak as a fool*] that is, if the equalling myself
to those false apostles would have been construed
as the vaunt of a fool, I will willingly be accounted
a greater fool, by taking place of them, and openly
pleading, that as to their ministry, I not only come
up even with them, but outstrip and go beyond
them: though this same commentator a little after,
as it were forgetting what he had just before delivered, tacks about and shifts to another interpretation.

But why do I insist upon any one particular example, when in general it is the public charter of all
divines, to mould and bend the sacred oracles till
they comply with their own fancy, spreading them
(as Heaven by its Creator) like a curtain, closing together, or drawing them back, as they please?   Thus
indeed St. Paul himself minces and mangles some
citations he makes use of, and seems to wrest them
to a different sense from what they were first intended for, as is confessed by the great linguist, St.
Hierom.   Thus when that apostle saw at Athens
the inscription of an altar, he draws from it an argument for the proof of the Christian religion; but
leaving out great part of the sentence, which perhaps
if fully recited might have prejudiced his cause, he

mentions only the two last words, viz., *Ignoto deo:
To the unknown God;* and this too not without
alteration, for the whole inscription runs thus: *To
the Gods of* Asia, Europe, *and* Africa, *to all foreign
and unknown Gods.*

'Tis an imitation of the same pattern, I will warrant you, that our young divines, by leaving out
four or five words in a place, and putting a false
construction on the rest, can make any passage serviceable to their own purpose; though from the co-
herence of what went before, or follows after, the
genuine meaning appears to be either wide enough,
or perhaps quite contradictory to what they would
thrust and impose upon it.* In which knack the
divines are grown now so expert, that the lawyers themselves begin to be jealous of an encroach-
ment upon what was formerly their sole privilege
and practice. And indeed what can they despair of
proving, since the fore-mentioned commentator (I
had almost blundered out his name, but that I am
restrained by fear of the same Greek proverbial sar-
casm) did upon a text of St. Luke put an interpretation, no more agreeable to the meaning of the
place, than one contrary quality is to another? The
passage is this, when Judas's treachery was prepar-
ing to be executed, and accordingly it seemed requisite that all the disciples should be provided to

---

*It is told of Archbishop Whately that when he heard of a bright
young curate taking for his text the words, "Hear the Church" (which
are cut out of the middle of a sentence, totally changing the meaning),
he said, "I should like to hear that gentleman preach a sermon on the
text, 'Hang all the law and the prophets.'"

guard and secure their assaulted master, our Saviour, that he might piously caution them against reliance for his delivery on any worldly strength, asks them, whether in all their embassy they lacked anything, when he had sent them out so unfurnished for the performance of a long journey, that they had not so much as shoes to defend their feet from the injuries of flints and thorns, or a scrip to carry a meal's meat in; and when they had answered that they lacked nothing, he adds, *But now he that hath a purse let him take it, and likewise a scrip; and he that hath no sword let him sell his garment, and buy one.* Now when the whole doctrine of our Saviour inculcates nothing more frequently than meekness, patience, and a contempt of this world, is it not plain what the meaning of the place is? Namely, that he might now dismiss his ambassadors in a more naked, defenceless condition, he does not only advise them to take no thought for shoes or scrip, but even commands them to part with the very clothes from their back, that so they might have the less incumbrance and entanglement in the going through their office and function. He cautions them, it is true, to be furnished with a sword, yet not such a carnal one as rogues and highwaymen make use of for murder and bloodshed, but with the sword of the Spirit, which pierces through the heart, and searches out the innermost retirements of the soul, lopping off all our lust and corrupt affections, and leaving nothing in possession of our breast but piety, zeal, and devotion: this (I say) in my opinion is the most

natural interpretation. But see how that divine mis-
understands the place; by sword (says he) is meant,
defence against persecution; by scrip, or purse, a
sufficient quantity of provision; as if Christ had, by
considering better of it, changed his mind in reference to that mean equipage, which he had before sent
his disciples in, and therefore came now to a recantation of what he had formerly instituted: or as if
he had forgot what in time past he had told them,
*Blessed are you when men shall revile you, and per-
secute you, and say all manner of evil against you
for my sake. Render not evil for evil,* for *blessed
are the meek,* not the cruel: as if he had forgot that
he encouraged them by the examples of sparrows
and lilies to take no thought for the morrow; he
gives them now another lesson, and charges them,
rather than go *without a sword, to sell their garment,
and buy one;* as if the going cold and naked were
more excusable than the marching unarmed. And
as this author thinks all means which are requisite
for the prevention or retaliation of injuries to be
implied under the name of sword, so under that of
scrip, he would have everything to be comprehended,
which either the necessity or conveniency of life requires.

Thus does this provident commentator furnish
out the disciples with halberts, spears, and guns, for
the enterprise of preaching Christ crucified; he supplies them at the same time with pockets, bags, and
portmanteaus, that they might carry their cupboards
as well as their bellies always about them: he takes

"Furnish out the disciples with halberts, spears, and guns, for the enterprise of preaching Christ crucified"

no notice how our Saviour afterwards rebukes Peter
for drawing that sword which he had just before so
strictly charged him to buy: nor that it is ever re-
corded that the primitive Christians did by no ways
withstand their heathen persecutors otherwise than
with tears and prayers, which they would have ex-
changed more effectually for swords and bucklers,
if they had thought this text would have borne them
out.

There is another, and he of no mean credit, whom
for respect to his person I shall forbear to name, who
commenting upon that verse in the prophet Habak-
kuk (*I saw the tents of Cushan in affliction, and the
curtains of the land of Midian did tremble*), because
tents were sometimes made of skins, he pretended
that the word tents did here signify the skin of St.
Bartholomew, who was flayed for a martyr.

I myself was lately at a divinity disputation
(where I very often pay my attendance), where one
of the opponents demanded a reason why it should
be thought more proper to silence all heretics by
sword and faggot, rather than convert them by mod-
erate and sober arguments?   A certain cynical old
blade, who bore the character of a divine, legible in
the frowns and wrinkles of his face, not without a
great deal of disdain answered, that it was the express injunction of St. Paul himself, in those directions to Titus (*A man that is an heretic, after the
first and second admonition, reject*), quoting it in
Latin, where the word *reject* is *devita*.   While all
the auditory wondered at this citation, and deemed

it no way applicable to his purpose; he at last explained himself, saying that *devita* signified *de vita
tollendum hereticum*, a heretic must be slain. Some
smiled at his ignorance, but others approved of it
as an orthodox comment. And however some disliked that such violence should be done to so easy
a text, our hair-splitting and irrefragable doctor
went on in triumph. To prove it yet (says he)
more undeniably, it is commanded in the old law
[*Thou shalt not suffer a witch to live*] : now then
every *Maleficus*, or witch, is to be killed, but an
heretic is *Maleficus*, which in the Latin translation
is put for a witch, *ergo, &c.* All that were present
wondered at the ingenuity of the person, and very
devoutly embraced his opinion, never dreaming that
the law was restrained only to magicians, sorcerers,
and enchanters: for otherwise, if the word *Maleficus*
signified what it most naturally implies, every evil-
doer, then drunkenness and whoredom were to meet
with the same capital punishment as witchcraft.
But why should I squander away my time in a too
tedious prosecution of this topic, which if drove on to
the utmost would afford talk to eternity? I aim
herein at no more than this, namely, that since those
grave doctors take such a swinging range and lati-
tude, I, who am but a smattering novice in divinity,
may have the larger allowance for any slips or mistakes.

Now therefore I return to St. Paul, who uses these
expressions [*Ye suffer fools gladly*], applying it to
himself; and again [*As a fool receive me*], and

The divinity disputation

[*That which I speak, I speak not after the Lord, but as it were foolishly*]: and in another place [*We are fools for Christ's sake*].   See how these commendations of Folly are equal to the author of them, both great and sacred.   The same holy person does yet enjoin and command the being a fool, as a virtue of all others most requisite and necessary: for, says he [*If any man seem to be wise in this world, let him become a fool, that he may be wise*].   Thus St. Luke records, how our Saviour, after his resurrection, joining himself with two of his disciples traveling to Emmaus, at his first salutation he calls them fools, saying [*O fools, and slow of heart to believe*].   Nor may this seem strange in comparison to what is yet farther delivered by St. Paul, who adventures to attribute something of Folly even to the all-wise God himself [*The foolishness of God (says he) is wiser than men*]: in which text St. Origen would not have the word foolishness any way referred to men, or applicable to the same sense, wherein is to be understood that other passage of St. Paul [*The preaching of the cross to them that perish, foolishness*].

But why do I put myself to the trouble of citing so many proofs, since this one may suffice for all, namely, that in those mystical psalms wherein David represents the type of Christ, it is there acknowledged by our Saviour, in way of confession, that even he himself was guilty of Folly; *Thou* (says he) *O God knowest my foolishness?* Nor is it without some reason that fools for their plainness and sincerity of heart have always been most acceptable to God Almighty. For the princes of this world have shrewdly suspected, and carried a jealous eye over such of their subjects as were the most observant, and deepest politicians (for thus Cæsar was afraid of the plodding Cassius and Brutus, thinking himself secure enough from the careless drinking Anthony; Nero likewise mistrusted Seneca, and Dionysius would have been willingly rid of Plato), whereas they can all put greater confidence in such as are of less subtlety and contrivance. So our Saviour in like manner dislikes and condemns the wise and crafty, as St. Paul does not obscurely declare in these words, *God hath chosen the foolish things of the world;* and again, *it pleased God by foolishness to save the world;* implying that by wisdom it could never have been saved. Nay, God himself testifies as much when he speaks by the mouth of his prophet, *I will destroy the wisdom of the wise, and bring to nought the understanding of the learned.* Again, our Saviour does solemnly return his Father thanks for that he had *hidden the mysteries of salvation from the wise, and revealed them to babes,* i.e., to fools. Now the Greek word for 'babes' is νηπίοις, being opposed to σοφοῖς; hence if one signify wise, the other must mean foolish. To the same purpose did our blessed Lord frequently condemn and upbraid the scribes, pharisees, and lawyers, while he carries himself kind and obliging to the unlearned multitude: for what otherwise can be the meaning of that tart denunciation, *Woe unto you scribes and*

pharisees, than woe unto you wise men, whereas he
seems chiefly delighted with children, women, and
illiterate fishermen.

We may farther take notice, that among all the
several kinds of brute creatures he shews greatest lik-
ing to such as are farthest distant from the subtlety
of the fox. Thus in his progress to Jerusalem he
chose to ride sitting upon an ass. though, if he
pleased, he might have mounted the back of a lion
with more of state, and as little of danger. The
Holy Spirit chose rather likewise to descend from
heaven in the shape of a simple gall-less dove, than
that of an eagle, kite, or other more lofty fowl.

Thus all along in the Holy Scriptures there are
frequent metaphors and similitudes of the most inoffensive creatures, such as stags, hinds, lambs, and
the like. Nay, those blessed souls that in the day
of judgment are to be placed at our Saviour's right
hand are called sheep, which are the most senseless
and stupid of all cattle, as is evidenced by Aristotle's
Greek proverb, προβάτειον ἦθος, a sheepishness of
temper, *i.e.,* a dull, blockish, sleepy, unmanly humour. Yet of such a flock Christ is not ashamed
to profess himself the shepherd. Nay, he would
not only have all his proselytes termed sheep, but
even he himself would be called a lamb; as when
John the Baptist seeth Jesus coming unto him, he
saith, *Behold the Lamb of God;* which same title is
very often given to our Saviour in the Apocalypse.

All this amounts to no less than that all mortal
men are fools, even the righteous and godly as well

as sinners; nay, in some sense our blessed Lord himself, who, although he was *the wisdom of the Father*, yet to repair the infirmities of fallen man, he became in some measure a partaker of human Folly, when he *took our nature upon him, and was found in fashion as a man;* or when God *made him to be sin for us, who knew no sin, that we might be made the righteousness of God in him.* Nor would he heal those breaches our sins had made by any other method than by the *foolishness of the cross*, published by the ignorant and unlearned apostles, to whom he frequently recommends the excellence of Folly, cautioning them against the infectiousness of wisdom, by the several examples he proposes them to imitate, such as children, lilies, sparrows, mustard, and such like beings, which are either wholly inanimate or at least devoid of reason and ingenuity, guided by no other conduct than that of instinct, without care, trouble, or contrivance. To the same intent the disciples were warned by their lord and master, that when they should be *brought unto the synagogues, and unto magistrates and powers*, they shall *take no thought how, or what thing they should answer, nor what they should say:* they were again strictly forbid to *enquire into the times and seasons*, or to place any confidence in their own abilities, but to depend wholly upon divine assistance.

At the first peopling of paradise the Almighty had never laid so strict a charge on our father Adam to refrain from *eating of the tree of knowledge* except he had thereby forewarned that the taste of know-

ledge would be the bane of all happiness. St. Paul
says expressly, that *knowledge puffeth up, i.e.,* it is
fatal and poisonous. In pursuance whereunto St.
Bernard interprets that *exceeding high mountain*
whereon the devil had erected his seat to have been the
mountain of knowledge. And perhaps this may be
another argument which ought not to be omitted,
namely, that Folly is acceptable, at least excusable,
with the gods, inasmuch, as they easily pass by the
heedless failures of fools, while the miscarriages of
such as are known to have more wit shall very
hardly obtain a pardon; nay, when a wise man
comes to sue for an acquitment from any guilt, he
must shroud himself under the patronage and pretext of Folly. For thus in the twelfth of Numbers
Aaron entreats Moses to stay the leprosy of his sister Miriam, saying, *alas, my Lord, I beseech thee
lay not the sin upon us, wherein we have done foolishly.* Thus, when David spared Saul's life, when
he found him sleeping in a tent of Hachilah, not
willing to *stretch forth his hand against the Lord's
anointed,* Saul excuses his former severity by confess-
ing, *Behold, I have played the fool, and have erred
exceedingly.* David also himself in much the same
form begs the remission of his sin from God Almighty with this prayer, *Lord, I pray thee take away
the iniquity of thy servant, for I have done very
foolishly;* as if he could not have hoped otherwise
to have his pardon granted except he petitioned for
it under the covert and mitigation of Folly. The
concordant practice of our Saviour is yet more con-

vincing, who, when he hung upon the cross, prayed for his enemies, saying, *Father, forgive them,* urging no other plea in their behalf than that of their ignorance, *for they know not what they do.* To the same effect St. Paul in his first epistle to Timothy acknowledges he had been a blasphemer and a persecutor, *But* (saith he) *I obtained mercy because I did it ignorantly in unbelief.* Now what is the meaning of the phrase [*I did it ignorantly*] but only this? My fault was occasioned from a misinformed Folly, not from a deliberate malice. What signifies [*I obtained mercy*] but only that I should not otherwise have obtained it had not folly and ignorance been my vindication? To the same purpose is that other passage in the mysterious Psalmist, which I forgot to mention in its proper place, namely, *Oh remember not the sins and offences of my youth!* The word which we render offences, is in Latin *ignorantias,* ignorances. Observe, the two things he alleges in his excuse are, first, his rawness of age, to which Folly and want of experience are constant attendants: and secondly, his ignorances, expressed in the plural number for an enhancement and aggravation of his foolishness.

But that I may not wear out this subject too far, to draw now towards a conclusion, it is observable that the Christian religion seems to have some relation to Folly, and no alliance at all with wisdom. Of the truth whereof, if you desire farther proof than my bare word, you may please, first, to con-

"Profusely lavish in their charity"

sider, that children, women, old men and fools, led
as it were by a secret impulse of nature, are always
most constant in repairing to church, and most
zealous, devout and attentive in the performance
of the several parts of divine service; nay, the first
promulgators of the Gospel, and the first converts
to Christianity, were men of plainness and simpli-
city, wholly unacquainted with secular policy or
learning.*

Farther, there are none more silly, or nearer their
wits' end, than those who are too superstitiously
religious: they are profusely lavish in their charity;
they invite fresh affronts by an easy forgiveness
of past injuries; they suffer themselves to be cheated
and imposed upon by laying claim to the innocence
of the dove; they make it the interest of no person
to oblige them, because they will love, and *do good
to their enemies,* as much as to the most endearing
friends; they banish all pleasure, feeding upon the
penance of watching, weeping, fasting, sorrow and
reproach; they value not their lives, but with St.
Paul, *wish to be dissolved,* and covet the fiery trial
of martyrdom: in a word, they seem altogether so
destitute of common sense that their soul seems
already separated from the dead and inactive body.
And what else can we imagine all this to be than
downright madness?   It is the less strange therefore
that at the feast of Pentecost the apostles should be

*The last phrase here is a notable toning down of what Erasmus
really says,—'*Acerrimos literarum hostes fuisse.*'

thought drunk with new wine; or that St. Paul was censured by Festus to have been beside himself.*

And since I have had the confidence to go thus far, I shall venture yet a little forwarder, and be so bold as to say thus much more: all that final happiness, which Christians, through so many rubs and briars of difficulties, contend for, is at last no better than a sort of folly and madness. This, no question, will be thought extravagantly spoken; but consider awhile, and deliberately state the case.

First, then, the Christians so far agree with the Platonists as to believe that the body is no better than a prison or dungeon for the confinement of the soul. That therefore, while the soul is shackled to the walls of flesh, her soaring wings are impeded, and all her enlivening faculties clogged and fettered by the gross particles of matter, so that she can neither freely range after, nor, when happily overtook, can quietly contemplate her proper object of truth.

Farther, Plato defines philosophy to be the meditation of death, because the one performs the same office with the other; namely, withdraws the mind from all visible and corporeal objects; therefore while the soul does patiently actuate the several organs and members of the body, so long is a man accounted

*These paragraphs prove (as do countless other exquisite touches in his writings) that Erasmus was a deep-souled Christian, and that his antipathy to so much in the Church was due to the anti-Christianity prevailing in it.

of a good and sound disposition; but when the soul, weary of her confinement, struggles to break jail, and fly beyond her cage of flesh and blood, then a man is censured at least for being maggoty and crack-brained; nay, if there be any defect in the external organs it is then termed downright madness. And yet many times persons thus affected shall have prophetic ecstasies of foretelling things to come, shall in a rapture talk languages they never before learned, and seem in all things actuated by somewhat divine and extraordinary; and all this, no doubt, is only the effect of the soul's being more released from its engagement to the body, whereby it can with less impediment exert the energy of life and motion.   From hence, no question, has sprung an observation of like nature, confirmed now into a settled opinion, that *some souls long experienced in the world, before their dislodging, arrive to the height of prophetic spirits.*

If this disorder arise from an intemperance in religion, and too high a strain of devotion, though it be of a somewhat different sort, yet it is so near akin to the former, that a great part of mankind apprehend it as a mere madness; especially when persons of that superstitious humour are so pragmatical and singular as to separate and live apart as it were from all the world beside: so as they seem to have experienced what Plato dreams to have happened between some, who, enclosed in a dark cave, did only ruminate on the ideas and abstracted speculations of entities; and one other of their company,* who had got abroad into the open light, and at his return tells them what a blind mistake they had lain under; that he had seen the substance of what their dotage of imagination reached only in shadow; that therefore he could not but pity and condole their deluding dreams, while they on the other side no less bewail his frenzy, and turn him out of their society for a lunatic and madman.

Thus the vulgar are wholly taken up with those objects that are most familiar to their senses, beyond which they are apt to think all is but fairyland; while those that are devoutly religious scorn to set their thoughts or affections on any things below, but mount their soul to the pursuit of incorporeal and invisible beings. The former, in their

---

*The immortal passage describing the fate of the lonely exile—'*fugitivo illi*'—from the cave, upon his return, is thus rendered into quaint Latin by Erasmus (or his commentator), in a note on the original text: 'Quod si unus illorum sordentium in specu, per aspera saxa atque ardua sursum traheretur, videretque apud superos solem et alias res veras, sicque postea ad pristinum specum reverteretur, putaret haud dubie illos, qui apud eos, qui in specu sedent, in summo honore essent, miserrimos esse. Ad hæc dicit, illum reversum iam in specum nihil visurum, propterea quod repente ex clarissimo sole in profundissimas tenebras veniret; et idcirco cum nihil umbrarum videret, omnibus in specu sedentibus risui fore, explosumque iri, simul atque de rebus veris disputare inciperet, tanquam stultum, et apud superos corruptum.'

It is always a joy to re-read it. and the purchasers of a limited edition will perhaps pardon the seeming pedantry which prompts the Editor to place it before them in this (to him) novel form.

marshalling the requisites of happiness, place riches in the front, the endowments of the body in the next rank, and leave the accomplishments of the soul to bring up the rear; nay, some will scarce believe there is any such thing at all as the soul, because they cannot with their bodily eyes see a reason of their faith; while the other pay their first fruits of service to that most simple and incomprehensible Being, God, employ themselves next in providing for the happiness of that which comes nearest to their immortal soul, being not at all mindful of their corrupt bodily carcases, and slighting money as the dirt and rubbish of the world; or if at any time some urging occasions require them to become entangled in secular affairs, they do it with regret, and a kind of ill-will, observing what St. Paul advises his Corinthians, *having wives, and yet being as though they had none; buying, and yet remaining as though they possessed not.*

There are between these two sorts of persons many differences in several other respects. As first, though all the senses have the same mutual relation to the body, yet some are more gross than others; as those five corporeal ones, of touching, hearing, smelling, seeing, tasting, whereas some again are more refined, and less adulterated with matter; such are the memory, the understanding, and the will. Now the mind will be always most ready and expedite at that to which it is naturally most inclined.

Hence is it that a pious soul, employing all its power and abilities in the pressing after such things as are farthest removed from sense, is perfectly stupid and brutish in the management of any worldly affairs; while on the other side, the vulgar are so intent upon their business and employment, that they have not time to bestow one poor thought upon a future eternity. From such ardour of divine meditation was it that Saint Bernard in his study drank oil instead of wine, and yet his thoughts were so taken up that he never observed the mistake.

Farther, among the passions of the soul, some have a greater communication with the body than others; as lust, the desire of meat and sleep, anger, pride, and envy; with these the pious man is in continual war, and irreconcilable enmity, while the vulgar cherish and foment them as the best comforts of life.

There are other affections of a middle nature, common and innate to every man; such are love to one's country, duty to parents, love to children, kindness to friends, and such like; to these the vulgar pay some respect, but the religious endeavour to supplant and eradicate from their soul, except they can raise and sublimate them to the most refined pitch of virtue; so as to love or honour their parents, not barely under that character (for what did they do more than generate a body? nay, even for that we are primarily beholden to God, the first parent of all mankind), but as good men only, upon whom is imprinted the lively image of that divine nature, which they esteem as the chief and only good, beyond whom nothing deserves to be beloved, nothing desired.

By the same rule they measure all the other offices or duties of life; in each of which, whatever is earthly and corporeal, shall, if not wholly rejected, yet at least be put behind what faith makes the *substance of things not seen.* Thus in the sacraments, and all other acts of religion, they make a difference between the outward appearance or body of them, and the more inward soul or spirit. As to instance, in fasting, they think it very ineffectual to abstain from flesh, or debar themselves of a meal's meat (which yet is all the vulgar understand by this duty), unless they likewise restrain their passions, subdue their anger, and mortify their pride; that the soul being thus disengaged from the entanglement of the body, may have a better relish to spiritual objects, and take an antepast of heaven. Thus (say they) in the holy Eucharist, though the outward form and ceremonies are not wholly to be despised, yet are these prejudicial, at least unprofitable, if as bare signs only they are not accompanied with the thing signified, which is *the death of Christ,* which we are hereby to represent by the vanquishing and burying our animal affections, that they may arise to a newness of life, and be united first to each other, then all to Christ.

These are the actions and meditations of the truly pious person: while the vulgar place all their religion in crowding up close to the altar, in listening to the words of the priest, and in being very circumspect at the observance of each trifling ceremony. Nor is it in such cases only as we have here given for instances, but through his whole course of life, that the pious man, without any regard to the baser materials of the body, spends himself wholly in a fixed intentness upon things spiritual, invisible, and eternal.

Now since these persons stand off, and keep at so wide a distance between themselves, it is customary for them both to think each other mad: and were I to give my opinion to which of the two the name does most properly belong, I should, I confess, adjudge it to the religious; of the reasonableness whereof you may be farther convinced if I proceed to demonstrate what I formerly hinted at, namely, that that ultimate happiness which religion proposes is no other than some sort of madness.

First, therefore, Plato dreamed somewhat of this nature when he tells us that the madness of lovers was of all other dispositions of the body most desirable: for he who is once thoroughly smitten with this passion, lives no longer within himself, but has removed his soul to the same place where he has

settled his affections, and loses himself to find the
object he so much dotes upon: this straying now,
and wandering of a soul from its own mansion,
what is it better than a plain transport of madness?
What else can be the meaning of those proverbial
phrases, *non est apud se,* he is not himself; *ad te redi,*
recover yourself; and *sibi redditus est,* he is come
again to himself?   And accordingly as love is more
hot and eager, so is the madness thence ensuing more
incurable, and yet more happy.   Now what
shall be that future happiness of glorified saints,
which pious souls here on earth so earnestly groan
for, but only that the spirit, as the more potent and
prevalent victor, shall overmaster and swallow up
the body; and that the more easily, because while
here below, the several members, by being mortified,
and kept in subjection, were the better prepared for
this separating change; and afterward the spirit itself
shall be lost, and drowned in the abyss of beatific
vision, so as the whole man will be then perfectly beyond all its own bounds, and be no otherwise happy
than as, transported into ecstasy and wonder, it feels
some unspeakable influence from that omnipotent
Being, which makes all things completely blessed, by
assimilating them to his own likeness.

Now although this happiness be then only consummated, when souls at the general resurrection
shall be re-united to their repristinate bodies, and
both be clothed with immortality; yet because a

religious life is but a continued meditation upon, and as it were a foreshadowing of the joys of heaven, therefore to such persons there is allowed some relish and foretaste of that pleasure here, which is to be their reward hereafter. And although this indeed be but a small pittance of satisfaction compared with that future inexhaustible fountain of blessedness, yet does it abundantly over-balance all worldly delights, were they all in conjunction set off to their best advantage; so great is the precedency of spiritual things before corporeal, of invisible before material and visible. This is what the prophet gives an eloquent description of, where he says by way of encouragement, that *eye hath not seen, nor ear heard, nor hath it entered into the heart of man to conceive those things which God hath prepared for them that love him.* This likewise is that better part which Mary chose, which shall not be taken from her, but perfected and completed by her mortal putting on immortality.

Now those who are thus devoutly affected— though few there are so—undergo somewhat of strange alteration, which very nearly approaches to madness; they speak many things at an abrupt and incoherent rate, as if they were actuated by some possessing daimon; they make an inarticulate noise, without any distinguishable sense or meaning; they sometimes screw and distort their faces to uncouth and antic looks; at one time beyond measure cheerful,

then as immoderately sullen; now sobbing, then
laughing, and soon after sighing, as if they were
perfectly distracted, and out of their senses. If they
have any sober intervals of coming to themselves
again, like St. Paul they then confess, that *they
were caught up they know not where, whether in
the body, or out of the body, they cannot tell;* as if
they had been in a dead sleep or trance, they remember nothing of what they have heard, seen, said, or
done: this they only know, that their past delusion
was a most desirable happiness; that therefore they
bewail nothing more than the loss of it, nor wish for
any greater joy than the quick return and perpetua-
tion of such madness. And this (as I have said) is
the foretaste or anticipation of future blessedness.

But I doubt I have forgot myself, and have already transgressed the bounds of modesty. However, if I have said anything too confidently or im-
pertinently, be pleased to consider that it was spoke
by Folly, and that under the person of a woman;
yet at the same time remember the applicableness of
that Greek proverb:

A fool oft speaks a seasonable truth:

Unless you will be so witty as to object that this
makes no apology for me, because the word ἀνήϱ
signifies a man, not a woman, and consequently my
sex debars me from the benefit of that observation.

I perceive now, that for a concluding treat you
expect a formal epilogue, and the summing up of

all in a brief recitation; but I will assure you, you are grossly mistaken if you suppose that after such a hodge-podge medley of speech I should be able to recollect anything I have delivered. Beside, as it is an old proverb, μισῶ μνάμοναν συμπόταν: *I hate a pot-companion with a good memory;* so indeed I may as truly say, μισῶ μνάμοναν ἀκροατήν: *I hate a hearer that will carry any thing away with him.* Wherefore, in short:—

> *Farewell! live long, drink deep, be jolly,*
> *Ye most illustrious votaries of Folly!*

FINIS.

"Mighty happy in that they can call the king master, and be allowed the familiarity of talking with him"